Second-Class Citizen

Buchi Emecheta was born of Ibuza parentage in Lagos, Nigeria. She came to England in 1962, since when she has lived in North London with her five children. She is a sociology graduate of London University and her writing includes radio and television plays, numerous articles for learned journals and magazines, eight novels (*In the Ditch, Second-Class Citizen, The Bride Price, The Slave Girl, The Joys of Motherhood, Destination Biafra, Naira Power* and *Double Yoke*), and four children's books (*Titch the Cat, Nowhere to Play, The Moonlight Bride, The Wrestling Match*). Her autobiography, *Head Above Water*, was published in December 1986. In 1980, she was appointed Senior Research Fellow in the Department of English and Literary Studies at the University of Calabar, Nigeria.

She is a member of the Advisory Council to the British Home Secretary on race and equality, and serves on the Arts Council of Great Britain.

She was selected as one of 1983's Best Young British Writers and is winner of several Literary Prizes including the *New Statesman* Jock Campbell Award.

Buchi Emecheta

Second-Class Citizen

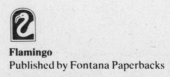

Flamingo
Published by Fontana Paperbacks

First published by Allison and Busby Ltd 1974
First issued in Fontana Paperbacks 1977
Fifth impression March 1982

This Flamingo edition first published
in February 1987 by Fontana Paperbacks,
8 Grafton Street, London W1X 3LA

Flamingo is an imprint of
Fontana Paperbacks, part of
the Collins Publishing Group

Made and printed in Great Britain by
William Collins Sons & Co. Ltd, Glasgow

Contents

To my dear children,
Florence, Sylvester, Jake, Christy and Alice,
without whose sweet background noises
this book would not have been written.

from the material made into a frock for her. She still remembered the frock; it was so big for her that she more or less swam into it. Her mother would never dream of making her a dress that was exactly her size because, you see, she would soon outgrow it. So even though she was a small girl, too skinny for her age, whatever that might be, she always had dresses three or four sizes bigger. That was one of her reasons for liking old dresses, since by the time her dresses were old, they fitted her. She was so happy with this new 'Lawyer dress' that she begged her mother to let her go with the women to the Apapa Wharf on the great day. It pained her so much when she realized that she was not going to be allowed to go because it fell on a school day.

School – the Ibos never played with that! They were realizing fast that one's saviour from poverty and disease was education. Every Ibo family saw to it that their children attended school. Boys were usually given preference, though. So even though Adah was about eight, there were still discussions about whether it would be wise to send her to school. Even if she was sent to school, it was very doubtful whether it would be wise to let her stay long. 'A year or two would do, as long as she can write her name and count. Then she will learn to sew.' Adah had heard her mother say this many times to her friends. Soon, Adah's younger brother, Boy, started school.

It was at this time that Adah's dream started to nudge her. Whenever she took Boy to Ladi-Lak Institute, as the school was called, she would stand by the gate and watch all her friends lining up by the school door, in their smart navy-blue pinafores looking clean and orderly. Ladi-Lak was then, and still is, a very small preparatory school. Children were not taught Yoruba or any African language. This was why it was such an expensive school. The proprietress was trained in the United Kingdom. At that time, more than half the children in the school were Ibos, as they were then highly motivated by the middle-class values. Adah would stand there, filled with envy. The envy later gave way to frustration, which she showed in many small ways. She would lie, just for the joy of lying; she took secret joy in disobeying her mother. Because, she thought to herself: *If not for Ma, Pa would have seen to it that I started school with Boy.*

One afternoon, Ma was sitting on the veranda of their house in Akinwunmi Street. With Adah's help, she had cooked the afternoon meal and they had both eaten. Ma started to undo her hair, ready to have it re-plaited. Adah had seen her do this a million times and was bored with watching her. There was nothing for her to do, there was nobody to play with; there was not even any mischief to plan. Then the thought suddenly struck her. Yes, she would go to school. She would not go to Ladi-Lak, because Boy was there and they might ask her to pay, it being such an expensive school. She would go to the Methodist School round the corner. It was cheaper, her Ma had said that she liked the uniform, most of her friends attended it, and Mr Cole, the Sierra Leonian neighbour living next door to them, taught there. Yes, she would go there.

Her dress was clean enough, though it was too big, but she thought of something to smarten it up. She went into their room, got an old scarf, twisted it round and round, so much so that it looked like a palm-tree climber's rope, then tied it round her little waist, pulling her baggy dress up a little. Other children went to school with slates and pencils. She had none. It would look ridiculous for her to march into a classroom without a slate and pencil. Then another thought struck her. She had always watched Pa shave: Pa had a broken slate, on which he usually sharpened a funny sort of curved knife. Adah often watched him do this, fascinated. After sharpening the knife, Pa would rub some carbolic soap lather on his chin and then would shave away. Adah thought of this slate. But the trouble was that it was so small. Just a small piece. It would not take many letters, but a small bit of slate was better than no slate at all. She then slipped it into the top of her dress, knowing full well that her scarf-belt would hold it up. Luck was with her. Before she left the room, one of Ma's innumerable friends came for a visit, and the two women were so engrossed in their chit-chat that they did not notice when Adah slipped past them.

Thus Adah went to school. She ran as fast as she could before anyone could stop her. She did not see any of Ma's

10

friends, because it was past midday and very hot; most people were too tired to walk the streets at this time. She got tired running and she started to trot like a lame horse; tired of trotting, she walked. She was soon at the schoolroom. There were two buildings in the compound. One was the church, and she had heard from her friends that the church was never used as a classroom. She knew which was the church because, even though she had not started school, she attended Sunday school in the church. With her head up, in determination, she walked down the centre looking for Mr Cole's class. This was easy for her because all the classes were separated from each other by low cardboard-like partitions. It was easy to see all the classes by simply walking down the middle.

When she saw Mr Cole, she walked into his class and stood behind him. The other children looked up from their work and stared at Adah in wonder. At first there was a hush, a hush so tangible that one could almost hold and feel it. Then one silly child started to giggle and the others followed suit, until almost every child in the class was giggling in such an uncontrollable way that Mr Cole glared at the children who had all gone crazy, for all he knew. Then it happened. The child who started the giggle covered her mouth with one hand and pointed at Adah with the other.

Mr Cole was a huge African, very young, very handsome. He was a real black man. His blackness shone like polished black leather. He was a very quiet man, but he used to smile at Adah every time he passed her on his way to school. Adah was sure Mr Cole would give her that reassuring smile now, in front of all these giggling idiots. Mr Cole spun round with such alacrity, that Adah took a step backwards. She was not frightened of Mr Cole, it was just that the movement was so quick and so unexpected of Mr Cole, with his great bulk. Only God above knew what he expected to find behind him. A big gorilla or a wandering 'masquerade' perhaps. But all he saw was Adah, staring at him.

God bless Mr Cole. He did not laugh, he took in the situation immediately, gave Adah one of those special smiles, held out his hand, and led her to a boy who had craw-craw on his head, and gestured her to sit down. Adah did not know what to make of this gesture. She felt Mr Cole should

have asked her why she came, but being reassured by his
smile, she said in her little loud voice:

'I came to school – my parents would not send me!'

The class went quiet once more, the boy with the craw-
craw on his head (he later became a lecturer in Lagos City
Hospital) gave her a bit of his pencil, and Adah scribbled
away, enjoying the smell of craw-craw and dried sweat. She
never forgot this smell of school.

The day ended too soon for Adah's liking. But they must
go home, Mr Cole assured her. Yes, of course she could come
again if she liked, but if her parents would not allow her to
come he would take it upon himself to teach her the alpha-
bet. If only Mr Cole would not bring her parents into it. Pa
would be all right: he would probably cane her, you know,
just a few strokes – six or so, not much – but Ma would not
cane, she would smack and smack, and then nag and nag
all day long.

She thought that it was these experiences with Ma so early
in life that had given her such a very low opinion of her
own sex. Somebody said somewhere that our characters
are usually formed early in life. Yes, that somebody was right.
Women still made Adah nervous. They had a way of sapping
her self-confidence. She did have one or two women friends
with whom she discussed the weather, and fashion. But when
in real trouble, she would rather look for a man. Men were
so solid, so safe.

Mr Cole took her to the stall of a woman selling *boli*,
which is the Yoruba name for roasted plantain. These women
usually had open pots in which they made a kind of coal
fire. These fires were covered with wire gauze; and on the
gauze were placed peeled plantains, ready for roasting. Mr
Cole fed her with a big *boli* and told her not to worry. It
was another story when they got home; at home things had
got out of hand.

In fact there was a big hullabaloo going on. Pa had been
called from work, Ma was with the police being charged with
child neglect, and the child that had caused all the fuss was
little Adah, staring at all of them, afraid and yet triumphant.
They took Ma to the police station and forced her to drink
a big bowl of *gari* with water. *Gari* is a tasteless sort of

flour made from cassava. When cooked and eaten with soup, it is delicious. But when uncooked, the watered type Ma was forced to drink, it became a torture, purgatorial in fact!

Those policemen! Adah still wondered where they got all their unwritten laws from. This happened at the police station near Sabo Market. Ma told them with tears in her eyes that she could swallow the *gari* no more. She must drink the whole lot, she was told, and told in such language that Adah hid behind Mr Cole. If Ma did not finish the *gari*, the policemen went on, they would take her to court. How they laughed at their own jokes, those horrid men; and how they scared Adah! Ma went on gulping, her eyes dilating. Adah was scared; she started to howl, and Pa, who had said very little, begged the policemen to stop. They should let Ma go now, he explained, for she had learnt her lesson. She was a great talker, very careless, otherwise Adah would not have been able to slip away as she had. Women were like that. They sat in the house, ate, gossiped and slept. They would not even look after their children properly. But the policemen should forgive her now, because Pa thought she had had enough *gari*.

The chief policeman considered this plea, then looked once more at Ma, cupping the *gari* to her mouth with her fingers, and smiled. He took pity on Ma, but warned her that if such a thing should happen again, he personally would take her to the court.

'You know what that means?' he thundered.

Ma nodded. She knew court meant two things: a heavy fine which she would never be able to afford, or prison, which she called 'pilizon'. They advised her to sell one of her colourful *lappas* and send Adah to school, because she looked like a child who was keen to learn. At this point Ma gave Adah a queer look – a look that contained a mixture of fear, love and wonder. Adah shrank back, still clutching Mr Cole.

When they got home from the station, the news had aready got round. Adah had nearly sent her mother to 'pilizon'. So frequently was this sentence repeated that Adah began to be quite proud of her impulsive move. She felt triumphant, especially when she heard Pa's friends advising him to make sure he allowed Adah to start school soon. This discussion took place on the veranda, where the visitors were downing two kegs of palm-wine to wet their parched throats. When they departed, Adah was left alone with her parents.

Things were not as bad as she thought they would be. Pa fished out the cane and gave her a few strokes for Ma's benefit. Adah did not mind that because they were not hard strokes. Maybe Pa had been mellowed by the talks with his friends, because when Adah cried after the caning, he came and talked to her seriously, just as if she were a grown up! He called her by her pet name, 'Nne nna', which means 'Father's mother', which was not so far from the meaning of Adah's real name. How she came by that name was a story in itself.

When Pa's mother was dying, she had promised Pa that she would come again, this time as his daughter. She was sorry she could not bring him up. She died when Pa was only five. She would come again, she had promised, to compensate for leaving him so young. Well, Pa grew up and married Ma at the Christ Church in Lagos, which was a Christian church. But Pa did not forget his mother's promise. The only reservation he had was that he did not want a girl for his first child. Well, his mother was impatient! Ma had a girl. Pa thought Adah was the very picture of his mother, even though Adah was born two months prematurely. He was quite positive that the little, damp monkey-like thing with unformed face was his 'come back mother'. So she was loaded with strings of names: 'Nne nna', 'Adah nna', 'Adah Eze'! Adah Eze means Princess, daughter of a king. Sometimes they called her Adah Eze, sometimes Adah nna and sometimes Nne nna. But this string of names was too long and too confusing for Adah's Yoruba friends and playmates and even more so for impatient Ma. So she became just 'Adah'. She didn't mind this. It was short: everybody could pronounce it. When she grew up, and was attending the Methodist Girls' High School in Lagos, where she came in contact with European missionaries, her name was one of the first ones they learned and pronounced correctly. This usually gave her a start against the other girls with long names like Adebisi Gbamgbose, or Oluwafunmilayo Olorunshogo!

✳

14

So that was how Adah started school. Pa would not hear of her going to the Methodist Primary; she was to go to the posh one, Ladi-Lak. Success in life would surely have come earlier to her if Pa had lived. But he died soon after, and Adah and her brother Boy were transferred to an inferior school. Despite all this, Adah's dream never left her.

It was understandable that Ma refused to take her to see the new lawyer, because Adah had started school only a few weeks before the preparations for the great man's arrival. Ma got really furious with Adah for asking such a thing.

'You made me drink *gari* only last month until I nearly burst my stomach, all because you said you wanted school. Now we gave you school, you want the wharf. No, you won't go. You chose school. To school you must go from now until you go grey.'

How right Ma was! Adah would never stop learning. She had been a student ever since.

Adah's face had fallen at this. If only she had known before, she would have staged her school drama after the arrival of Lawyer Nweze. But as it turned out, she missed little. The women practised their songs several times and showed off their uniform to which they had given the name *Ezidiji ji de ogoli, ome oba*, meaning: 'When a good man holds a woman she becomes a queen.' They wove the name of the uniform into the song, and it was a joy to hear and see these women, happy in their innocence, just like children. Their wants were simple and easily met. Not like those of their children who later got caught up in the entangled web of industrialization. Adah's Ma had no experience of having to keep up mortgage payments: she never knew what it was to have a family car, or worry about its innards; she had no worries about pollution, the population explosion or race. Was it surprising, therefore, that she was happy, being un-aware of the so-called joys of civilization and all its pit-falls?

They went to the wharf that day, these happy women, to welcome someone who had been to have a taste of that civilization; the civilization which was soon afterwards to hook them all, like opium. That day, they were happy to welcome their man.

They went in their new uniform. Adah still remembered
its colour. It had a dark velvety background with pale blue
drawings of feathers on it. The headscarf was red, and it
was tied in such a way that it displayed their straightened
hair. The shoes they wore were of black patent leather
called 'nine-nine'. No one really knew why, maybe it was
the rhythm of the repetition. In any case they wore those
'nine-nine' shoes with their '*Ezidiji ji de ogoli ome oba*' and
bought new gourds which they covered with colourful beads.
When these gourds were rattled, they produced sounds
like the Spanish samba, with a wild sort of animal over-
tone.

They had had a good time, Adah was told later. They danced
happily at the wharf, shaking their colourful gourds in the
air. The European arrivals gaped at them. They had never
seen anything like it before. The climax of it all was when
an Englishman took their photographs. He even singled out
women with babies on their backs and took several shots of
them. Ma and her friends were really happy to have their
pictures taken by Europeans! These were the days before
Nigerian independence when nearly every boat from England
brought hundreds of English graduates and doctors to work
in the schools and hospitals of Lagos.

The few gaps in the magical story of Nweze's arrival
were filled in by Pa. All the Ibuza men went to welcome him
the following Sunday. They could not leave their places of
work during the week. Pa said that the lawyer could not
swallow pounded yam any more; he could not even eat a
piece of bone. The meat they cooked for him had to be stewed
for days until it was almost a pulp. 'I felt like being sick,'
Pa said as he spat on the floor. 'It reminded me of the sickly,
watery food we ate in the army. There is one thing, though,'
Pa went on, 'he did not bring a white woman with him.'
All Pa's friends agreed with him that that was a good thing.
If Nweze had brought a white woman to Ibuza, Oboshi
would have sent leprosy on her!

Remembering all these taboos and superstitions of the
Western Ibos of Nigeria, Adah could not help laughing to
herself. She had been brought up with them, they were part
of her, yet now, in the seventies, the thought of them amused

16

her. The funniest thing about all these superstitions and beliefs was that they still had a doleful grip on the minds of her people. No one dared ignore any of them. Leprosy was a disease with which the goddess of the biggest river in Ibuza cursed anyone who dared to flout one of the town's traditions.

Well, Pa and his friends toasted the goddess of the River Oboshi for not allowing Lawyer Nweze to go astray. That Oboshi was strong enough to guide the thoughts of Nweze, demonstrated her power. They toasted her again.

Later, Adah did not know what came over that River Oboshi, though. Oil was discovered very near her, and she allowed the oilmen to dig into her, without cursing them with leprosy. The oilmen were mainly white, which was a surprise. Or perhaps she had long been declared redundant by the greater gods. That would not have surprised Adah, for everybody could be declared redundant these days, even goddesses. If not redundant, then she must have been in a Rip Van Winkle sleep, for she also allowed the Hausa soldiers to come and massacre her sons, and some Ibuza men had married white women without getting leprosy. Only last year an Ibuza girl graduate had married a white American! So Oboshi was faster than most of her sons and daughters at catching up with the times.

Anyway, the talk about Nweze's arrival went on for months and months. Adah talked about him to all her friends at school, telling them that he was her cousin. Well, everybody else talked big, so she might as well. But she made a secret vow to herself that she would go to this United Kingdom one day. Her arrival there would be the pinnacle of her ambition. She dared not tell anyone; they might decide to have her head examined or something. A small girl of her kind, with a father who was only a railwayman and a mother who knew nothing but the Ibo Bible and the Ibo Anglican hymn book, from the Introduction to the Index, and who still thought that Jerusalem was at the right hand of God.

That she would go to the United Kingdom one day was a dream she kept to herself, but dreams soon assumed substance. It lived with her, just like a Presence.

2 Escape into Elitism

Most dreams, as all dreamers know quite well, do have setbacks. Adah's dream was no exception, for hers had many.

The first hitch happened all of a sudden. Just a few months after she started school, Pa went to the hospital for something, she could not remember what. Then someone – she was not quite sure who it was – told her that Pa was staying there for a few days. A week or two later Pa was brought home, a corpse. After that things moved so fast that she sometimes got them confused. Adah, like most girl-orphans, was to live with her mother's elder brother as a servant. Ma was inherited by Pa's brother, and Boy was to live with one of Pa's cousins. It was decided that the money in the family, a hundred pounds or two, would be spent on Boy's education. So Boy was cut out for a bright future, with a grammar school education and all that. Adah's schooling would have been stopped, but somebody pointed out that the longer she stayed at school, the bigger the dowry her future husband would pay for her. After all, she was too young for marriage at the age of nine or so, and moreover the extra money she would fetch would tide Boy over. So, for the time being, Adah stayed at school.

Adah missed her old school, the cleanliness, the orderliness and the brightness, but she could not continue there. The fee was almost six times the cost of the others and she had to get herself used to an older and noisier school, otherwise she would not be allowed to go to school at all. But she had gained something from her short stay at Ladi-Lak, a very good and sound beginning, which put her ahead of her new class. Her efforts amused her cousins greatly – they regarded her as a funny little girl. She was glad, though, that they mercifully left her to dream after she had done her day's work.

The day's work! Jesus! Her day started at four-thirty in the morning. On the veranda of her new home in Pike Street, there was a mighty drum used as a water container and Adah had to fill this with water before going to school. This usually meant making ten to twelve trips to the public 'pump', as those public monstrosities were called in those days.

In Adah's new family there was Ma's brother who worked in the dockyard at the marina; his old wife, a quiet, retiring woman who was a shadow to her autocratic husband; and their four mighty sons, all grown up. One was married with a young daughter, one was working as a clerk in the Treasury, one was an artist, who would stay at home and sing all day long, the youngest was at a finishing school. So Pa's death was a blessing to them, for it meant they could have Adah as an unpaid servant to help in this bulging household. All these people occupied only one room and a veranda, yet the house had ten rooms! One could imagine the number of households that depended on the pump at Pike Street, for it served eight other streets as well. It was always a case of first come, first served. By seven or eight in the mornings there were usually fights, metal buckets were thrown in the air, fists drawn, and clothes torn. To avoid this rush hour, Adah was usually woken up at four-thirty. Her being up so early was also a great help to her new Pa and master. He went to work by six-thirty in the mornings and Adah had to be there to get him his odds and ends.

One might think on this evidence that Africans treated their children badly. But to Adah's people and to Adah herself, this was not so at all; it was the custom. Children, especially girls, were taught to be very useful very early in life, and this had its advantages. For instance, Adah learned very early to be responsible for herself. Nobody was interested in her for her own sake, only in the money she would fetch, and the housework she could do and Adah, happy at being given this opportunity of survival, did not waste time thinking about its rights or wrongs. She had to survive.

Time went by quickly, and when she reached the age of eleven, people started asking her when she was going to leave school. This was an urgent question because the fund for Boy's education was running low; Ma was not happy with

19

her new husband and it was considered time that Adah started making a financial contribution to her family. This terrified Adah. For a time it seemed as if she must give in to save Ma from the humiliating position she found herself in. She hated Ma for marrying again, thinking it was a betrayal of Pa. Sometimes she dreamt of marrying early; a rich man who would allow Ma and Boy to come and stay with her. That would solve a lot of problems, but the kind of men that she was being pushed to by her clever cousins and Ma's tactful hints were bald and huge, almost as big as her dead Pa. Ma had told her that older men took better care of their wives than the young and overeducated ones, but Adah didn't like them. She would never, never in her life get married to any man, rich or poor, to whom she would have to serve his food on bended knee: she would not consent to live with a husband whom she would have to treat as a master and refer to as 'Sir' even behind his back. She knew that all Ibo women did this, but she wasn't going to!

Unfortunately, her obstinacy gained her a very bad reputation; what nobody told her then was that the older men were encouraged to come and 'talk' to her because only they could afford the high 'bride-price' Ma was asking. Since, however, she didn't know this, as soon as she saw one of those 'baldies' in his white starched trousers, she would burst into native songs about bad old baldies. If that failed to repel them, she would go to the back yard and burst the bicycle tyres of the suitors. She discovered later this was very bad indeed, because she had since learnt that the Nigerian Government usually gave the junior clerks an advance for these bicycles. All the suitors were doing then was to ask for the advance for their new Raleigh bikes with flashy lights in order to impress Adah. But the stupid girl refused to be impressed.

The number of suitors did start to dwindle, though. Maybe word went round that she was a peculiar girl, for she did look funny in those days; all head, with odd-coloured hair and a tummy that would have graced any Oxfam poster. She was subsequently told that they stopped coming because she was cranky and ugly. She did not dispute that; she was ugly then, all skin and bone.

The thought of her having to leave school at the end of

the year worried her so much that she lost weight. She acquired a pathetically anxious look; the type some insane people have, with eyes as blank as contact lenses.

At about this time, something happened that showed her that her dream was just suffering a tiny dent, just a small one, nothing deep enough to destroy the basic structure. The dream by now assumed an image in her mind, it seemed to take life, to breathe and to smile kindly at her. The smile of the Presence became wide as the headmaster of Adah's school announced the lists of available secondary schools which the children could apply for. 'You are going, you must go and to one of the very best of schools; not only are you going, you're going to do well there,' Adah heard the Presence telling her. She heard it so much that she started to smile. The headmaster's voice jolted her back to reality.

'And what is it about me that you find so funny, Adah Ofili?'

'Me, sir? Oh, no, sir, I was not laughing, I mean not smiling, sir.'

'You were not what? You mean I am lying? Well, back her up!'

Immediately a group of three or four tough-looking boys came out from the back row and the biggest of them all swept Adah on to his back and two others held her feet while the headmaster administered the cane to her posterior. The searing of the cane was so intense that Adah was beyond screaming. To ease the pain, she sank her sharp teeth deep into the back of the poor boy who was backing her. He started to scream loudly, but Adah would not let go, not even when the caning stopped. The boy wriggled in agony and so did Adah. All the teachers came to the rescue. Adah's teeth had dug so deep into him that fragments of his flesh were stuck between her teeth. She quickly spat them out and wiped her mouth, looking at them all wide-eyed.

'You'll go to jail for this,' the headmaster thundered and he took the boy into his office for first aid. From that day on, no boy ever volunteered to back Adah up any more, but that incident gave her a nickname which she never lived down: the Ibo tigress. Some of her Yoruba classmates used to ask her what human flesh tasted like, because 'You Ibos used to eat people, didn't you?' Well, Adah didn't know about the cannibalistic tendencies of her tribe; all she knew was that the headmaster's cane burnt her so much that she felt irrepressible urges to pass the pain to something else. Latifu, the boy who was doing the backing, happened to be the closest victim, so he had to take it. Adah also felt that she was being unjustly punished. She had been smiling at the Presence, not the headmaster, and she suspected that the headmaster knew she was telling the truth; he had simply wanted to cane her, that was all.

Adah waited for days for the Law which the headmaster said was coming to take her to jail. No policemen came for her, so she decided that she had either been forgotten or that her bite of Latifu was not deep enough to merit imprisonment. The thought nagged her, though. It nagged her so much that she was tempted to commit another atrocity, this time a really horrible one that nearly sent her, not to jail, but to her Maker.

Adah was given two shillings to buy a pound of steak from a market called Sand Ground. She looked at the two-shilling piece for a very, very long time. All she needed to take the entrance examination to the school of her dreams was two shillings. Didn't Jesus say that one should not steal? But she was sure there was a place in the Bible where it said that one could be as clever as the serpent but as harmless as the dove. Would she be harming anybody if she paid for her entrance examination fee with this two shillings? Would Jesus condemn her for doing it: for stealing? After all, her cousin could afford the money, though he would not give it to her if she asked for it in the proper way. What was she to do? That was the trouble with Jesus, He never answered you; He never really gave you a sign of what to do in such a tempting situation. Anybody could twist what He said to suit his own interpretation. Then she saw the Image again. It was going to be all right, the Image was smiling, so Adah buried the money and went back home in tears, without the meat.

She was really no good at lying. The wildness in her eyes had a way of betraying her. If only she could have kept her large eyes lowered it would have been all right: people would have believed her story. But she kept staring into their eyes, and her face showed her up like a mirror.

'You're lying, Adah,' her cousin's wife said, pointedly.

Adah opened her mouth, but had to close it quickly, because no sound came. She knew what was going to happen to her; the cane. She did not mind this caning because she knew that anybody who sinned must be punished. What she did not bargain for was the extent of the punishment. Her cousin sent her out with a threepenny piece to buy the type of cane called the *koboko*. It was the one the Hausas used for their horses. There was nothing Adah could do but buy it. Her cousin warned her that he would not stop administering the cane until she'd told him the truth. That was bad thought Ada. She had to go to the Methodist Girls' High School or die. She concentrated her mind on something else. After the burning of the first few strokes, her skin became hardened, and so did her heart. She started to count. When Cousin Vincent had counted to fifty, he appealed to Adah to cry a little. If only she would cry and beg for mercy, he would let her go. But Adah would not take the bait. She began to see herself as another martyr; she was being punished for what she believed in. Meanwhile Cousin Vincent's anger increased; he caned her wildly, all over her body. After a hundred and three strokes, he told Adah that he would never talk to her again: not in this world nor in the world to come. Adah did not mind that. She was, in fact, very happy. She had earned the two shillings.

The headmaster at her school did not believe his ears when Adah told him that she was going to sit for the common entrance examination. He looked at her kwashiorkor-ridden body for a very long time then shrugged his shoulders. 'One can never tell with you Ibos. You're the greatest mystery the good God has created.' So he put her name down.

Sometimes the thought that she might not be able to pay the fees crossed her mind. But she did not let that worry her. She had read somewhere that there was some sort of scholarship for the five or so children who did best in the exam. She was going to compete for one of those places. She was so determined that not even the fact that her number was nine hundred and forty-seven frightened her. She was going to that school, and that was that!

But how was she to tell them at home? She had stopped liking Cousin Vincent. Every time she knelt down to pray, she used to tell God to send him to hell. She did not believe in that stuff of loving your enemy. After all, God did not like the Devil, so why should she pray for the man who had the heart to cane her for a good two hours with a *koboko*? When Cousin Vincent failed his Cambridge School Certificate examinations, Adah burst out laughing. God had heard her prayers.

The entrance examination was to take place on a Saturday. That was going to be very difficult. How was she to get away? Another lie? She could not do that again. She would be discovered, and they would stop her from taking the examination; so she told her uncle, Ma's brother, that she was going to sit for the examination. The funniest thing was that nobody even asked her where she got the money from. Nobody wanted to know. As long as she was not asking for money from anybody, and as long as she had done her Saturday job, she could go to the devil for all they cared!

Occasionally, the mother of the house, Ma's sister-in-law, would ask how she proposed to get the money for the school fees and remind her that her father was dead. In response, Adah's mind would flutter with fear, but she never told anyone she was dreaming of winning a scholarship. That was too big an ambition for a girl like her to express.

She was aware that nobody was interested in her since Pa died. Even if she had failed, she would have accepted it as one of the hurdles of life. But she did not fail. She not only passed the entrance examination. But she got a scholarship with full board. She never knew whether she came first or second or even third, but she was one of the best children that year.

Since then she had started to be overawed by the Presence. It existed right beside her, just like a companion. It comforted her during the long school holidays when she could not go home, because there was no home for her to go to.

She was very happy at the Methodist Girls' School especially during the first four years. However, a cloud of indecision started to loom when her school days were coming to an end. It was incredible how quickly five years could pass! She would have liked to linger there, in the boarding house; to stretch each day into a year and each year into a century. But that was impossible. The final day came and she was quite unprepared for life outside. She had some vague plans about what she was going to do; she was going to continue her education, she was going to go to Ibadan University to read Classics and she was going to teach at the end of it all.

Well, there was one thing she had not bargained for. To read for a degree, to read for the entrance examination, or even for more 'A' levels, one needed a home. Not just any home where there would be trouble today and fights tomorrow, but a good, quiet atmosphere where she could study in peace.

Adah could not find a home like that. In Lagos, at that time, teenagers were not allowed to live by themselves, and if the teenager happened to be a girl as well, living alone would be asking for trouble. In short, Adah had to marry.

Francis was a very quiet young man who was reading to be an accountant. Adah congratulated herself on her marriage. At least he was not an old baldy, neither was he a 'made man' then, though there was no doubt that he was going to be made one day. To Adah the greatest advantage was that she could go on studying at her own pace. She got great satisfaction, too, from the fact that Francis was too poor to pay five hundred pounds bride-price Ma and the other members of her family were asking. She was such an expensive bride because she was 'college trained', even though none of them had contributed to her education. The anger of her people was so intense that none of them came to her wedding.

That wedding itself was a hilarious affair. Francis and Adah were both under age, and the only witness, Francis's mother, had to sign with her thumb. The whole affair started off on the wrong foot. They had forgotten to buy a ring, and the skinny man with a black bow tie refused to marry them, even when Adah assured him that a piece of string would do until they got home.

'I've never heard of such a wedding!' the man declared, sweating in his tight collar.

'Please marry us without a ring because, you see, before we can get to Ebute-Metta, you will have closed for the day!' Adah begged.

'Never mind about that, you just come back tomorrow with a ring and I will marry you.'

They were married the following day. It was the saddest day in Adah's whole life. She did not mind having to go home in a bus, neither did she mind not marrying in white, which she hated anyway, but still she was sad, very sad, for months after the marriage at the register office.

Soon, however, things improved. Adah gave birth to a daughter and she and Francis were both delighted with the baby.

Then, after endless interviews and form fillings, Adah was selected to work as a librarian in the American Consulate Library at Campbell Street. The size of her pay packet worried Francis a little, and he had to ask his Pa for advice.

'Do you think our marriage will last if I allow Adah to go and work for the Americans? Her pay will be three times my own. My colleagues at work will laugh at me. What do you think I should do?'

'You are a fool of a man, you are. Where will she take the money to? Her people? Her people, who did not even come to congratulate her on the arrival of baby Titi? Her relatives, who did not care whether she lived or died? The money is for you, can't you see? Let her go and work for a million Americans and bring their money here, into this house. It is your luck. You made a good choice in marriage, son.'

Francis was as delighted as a schoolboy. Adah would have to be protected, especially on the pay days. On the first pay day, Adah was to be paid about sixty pounds or so. Neither Adah nor Francis had ever seen such a fantastic sum. It was decided that Francis should work only a half day in his office, and then take a bus to meet Adah, in order to be a bodyguard for his wife and their money. Both husband and wife carried the money to Tinubu Square in Adah's work

26

bag like a delicate baby. They talked about their plans for this sudden prosperity.

'We are ahead of all our colleagues, you know,' Francis remarked.

'God is wonderful! Fancy me earning such a fantastic sum. Our new baby is going to be very lucky.'

'If he happens to be a boy we'll call him Kennedy.'

'And if a girl, we'll call her Jacqueline.'

There was a long pause during which the young couple eyed a man in an *agbada* robe suspiciously.

'Some of these rogues do smell money, you know,' Francis whispered.

'Yes, I know,' nodded Adah.

Francis clutched the raffia bag tightly to his chest, and frowned in the direction of the unsuspecting man.

'I have been thinking,' Adah said, all of a sudden. 'I used to dream that one day I would go to the United Kingdom. Why don't we save and go, now that we shall be able to afford it? We can take our children with us. Everybody goes to the United Kingdom now. I'll be glad if we can go too.'

The smile on Francis's face was like a warm sunshine after a thunderous rain. It spread from ear to ear on his beardless face. He would be very happy if they could make it. He would finish his accountancy and Adah would read librarianship. He would go first, and Adah would send him twenty pounds every month; she was to save her fare and that of the children, she was to feed herself and the children whilst they were still in Lagos and pay the rent and help in paying the school fees of Francis's seven sisters.

Adah did not mind in the least being saddled with all these responsibilities even though her bride-price had not been paid. It never occurred to her to save her new high salary for her bride-price. She knew that all she did would go towards making her young family into a family of Ibo élites, just like Lawyer Nweze of Ibuza, who by then had become a Minister in Northern Nigeria. That lawyer was a funny man, Adah thought. He did not come to the South, to Ibuza, to give the people of the town electricity, nor did he come to worship the River Oboshi. He just stayed put in the North making barrels and barrels of money. When

Adah was still at the American Consulate news appeared in the Nigerian papers that Lawyer Nweze was defending a Hausa multi-millionaire. They said the millionaire was so rich that he had a railway line built right down to his palace door. The man had eight Rolls-Royces. After the case Nweze ended up a millionaire himself. Adah still wondered how that happened, because the millionaire was jailed for forging notes in his great palace. Francis and Adah sometimes wondered what he had paid Nweze with.

In any case that was Nweze's headache, not Adah Obi's! As far as she was concerned, her dreams were all coming true. Her marriage was less than eighteen months old, yet she already had four maids, two were paid three pounds each, the other two were paid their fees for secondary schools. These two, Cecilia and Angelina, were Francis's sisters. These four girls did all the work in the house. All Adah had to do was to go to the American library, work till two-thirty, come home and be waited on hand and foot, and in the evening be made love to. She did not disappoint her parents-in-law on that score. For, apart from the fact that she earned enough money to keep them all going, she was very prolific which, among the Ibos, is still the greatest asset a woman can have. A woman would be forgiven everything as long as she produced children. Adah was so fast on this score that she was given the nickname 'Touch Not' among the other wives of her age group. 'As soon as her husband touches her, she gets a swollen tummy,' they used to laugh.

Later, in England, writing about that time of her life almost with nostalgia, she used to ask herself why she had not been content with that sort of life, cushioned by the love of her parents-in-law, spoilt by her servants and respected by Francis's younger sisters. As for her mother-in-law, she was everything that Ma was not: quiet, beautiful, and motherly. Some of Adah's friends used to think that she was Adah's real mother, they were so close. But she suspected somewhere in her heart that the contentment she had then was superficial. She did not know her husband very well because, as most young African wives know, most of the decisions about their own lives had to be referred first to Big Pa, Francis's

28

father, then to his mother, then discussed amongst the brothers of the family before Adah was referred to. She found all this ridiculous, the more so if the discussion involved finance. After all, she would have to pay for the plan in most cases but the decision would have been made behind her back. Of course Francis was simply a puppet in such cases, and so was she. They could not refuse. They had to bow down to their elders.

Elders or no elders, they were going to live their own lives. It would have been fairer if some of the elders were from her own side of the family. But both Adah's parents were dead by then. Ma had died, aged thirty-eight, when Adah was in hospital having Titi, so she felt cheated in a way.

Cheated by the fact that neither her Pa nor Ma had lived to see any of her children; cheated by the fact that she was bringing so much joy into her husband's house and none into hers. Boy never visited her, neither did any of her cousins and uncles. They felt Adah had let them down. They said Adah should have continued her education and become a doctor since she had managed to struggle through secondary school. But nobody talked of who was going to support her, nobody talked of where she was going to live. So she found herself alone once more, forced into a situation dictated by society in which, as an individual, she had little choice. She would rather that she and her husband, whom she was beginning to love, moved to new surroundings, a new country and among new people. So she said special prayers to God, asking Him to make Pa agree to their going to the land of her dreams, the United Kingdom! Just like her Pa, she still said the name United Kingdom in a whisper, even when talking to God about it, but now she felt it coming nearer to her. She was beginning to believe she would go to England.

Francis broke the good news to her one day after their evening meal. Pa had agreed, he said. Adah was so full of happiness that she started to dance an African calypso. So they were going at last! She was soon going to be called 'been-to', which was a Lagos phrase for those who had 'been to' England. Francis allowed her to finish before he dropped the bomb-shell.

'You know how old-fashioned Father is.'

Adah knew and nodded, startled by her husband's grave tones.

'Father does not approve of women going to the UK. But you see, you will pay for me, and look after yourself, and within three years, I'll be back. Father said you're earning more than most people who have been to England. Why lose your good job just to go and see London? They say it is just like Lagos.'

Francis was an African through and through. A much more civilized man would probably have found a better way of saying this to his wife. But to him, he was the male, and he was right to tell her what she was going to do. Adah, from the day of her registry marriage, had seen the romantic side of her life being shattered, like broken glass, about her. Francis had had a very expensive education at Hussey College in Warri, but his outlook on life was pure African. He had had little opportunity of coming in contact with Europeans as Adah had. Those God-forsaken missionaries! They had taught Adah all the niceties of life, they taught her by the Bible, where a woman was supposed to be ready to give in to her man at any time, and she was to be much more precious to her husband than rubies. It was all right for a man who had seen rubies before and knew their worth. What of a man who would throw rubies away, thinking that they were useless stones? What was she to do now? Cry? It was too late. Who were these people anyway? Illiterate parents, who thought they knew a great deal of a curious kind of philosophy by which she was not going to bring up her children. There was no point in arguing with Francis, there was no need to ask him who he thought he was. He would not understand. 'Be as cunning as a serpent but as harmless as a dove,' she quoted to herself. So she was to stay in Nigeria, finance her husband, give his parents expensive gifts occasionally, help in paying the school fees for some of the girls, look after her young children and what then, rot? So this was where her great dream had led her. She should have married one of the baldies. It was too late now, not even a baldy would have her. All she had to do was to change the situation, and that she was determined to do. She pretended to be all for the plan. Of course she would stay in Lagos and look after the family; of course she would send him money regularly and, if possible, move in with her mother-in-law. Francis was not to worry about her at all, everything was going to work out well.

'My father told me I made a right decision the day I said I was going to marry you. You know what he told me? No? I'll tell you. He said to me, "Adah trained herself. She learnt very early to let her common sense guide her. She has the makings of a woman who would think before she acts. Very few women can do that, I tell you." '

They both burst out laughing.

'Father was right, was he not?' Francis wanted to be re-assured.

Yes, your father was more right than he knew, Adah thought to herself. First of all Francis must go, then she would get down to work on her in-laws, and work on them very hard until they let her go.

Plans for Francis's departure were soon under way. He got together everything he needed in no time at all. It cost Adah a small fortune though, because it was bribery all the way through. To get a passport in those days, one had to bribe even the messenger at the passport ᵥffice. Curiously enough, the office was manned by policemen. Even the man at the top, whose fee was twenty pounds, was a policeman. All his subordinates were paid five pounds each. Francis and Adah lived on Francis's income, and spent all Adah's on the preparation for his departure.

The night before he left Nigeria, Francis took a group photograph with his family and Adah's little girl. Adah refused to pose for the photograph. She did not know why, but just did not wish to appear in it. Maybe it was because she was too big with the new child, but she knew the photographer could have cleverly disguised that! A relative of theirs came to make a special prayer to the River Oboshi. Some pieces of kolanut were brought by Francis's mother, and these were broken by the relative, then they were thrown into a circle on the floor, drawn with a chalk. A long prayer was sung to the goddess, who was four hundred miles away in Ibuza. She was requested to guide Francis, to keep him from the evil eye of white girls, to make him pass his examinations in good time, to bless him with all the money in England, to bless him with everything that was good in England; she was requested especially to forget him when circulating diseases and anything plaguey. This confused Adah. Was Oboshi responsible for the lives of people in England too? she wondered. In any case, at the end of it all, they were all ordered to eat the pieces of kolanut, which they munched with great satisfaction.

That was the trouble with being a believer in all these transcendent Beings. One did not know when one aroused the anger of one or the other. For instance, did their chewing of the kolanuts offered to Oboshi automatically make them the enemies of Jehovah?

Well, Adah debated with herself, Oboshi being such a powerful goddess might be able to protect them from the wrath of other gods. But Adah's being a Christian complicated the issue all the more. Didn't the God of the Christians, whom Adah believed in, tell Moses somewhere that he was a jealous God 'visiting the iniquity of fathers upon the children unto the third and fourth generation of them that hate me'? That God would hate them for chewing those pieces of kolanut, Adah was sure. Nothing would deaden her guilty conscience; not even the fact that her mother-in-law, who was a devout Catholic, bought the kolanuts, nor the fact that she was munching away happily herself. Adah looked at Francis, who carried the Bible every weekend, telling people the 'good news of the kingdom' from a two-penny magazine called the *Watchtower*. Well, it was all right for her mother-in-law – she would quickly go to the padre, who lived round the corner at St Paul's church and confess it all to him. The padre would then give her absolution. That would free her conscience to sin again if she liked. As for Francis, he became a Jehovah's Witness whenever he felt like it, or when he could use it as an excuse for being selfish. When Adah was ill with the first baby, Francis had given his blood to save her life, forgetting that the Witnesses were not supposed to do that. When he was busy with his preparation for coming to England, he forgot his *Watchtower* and *Awake*. He also forgot that coming to England was seeking after materialism which he preached to Adah was not only evil but unnecessary, because Armageddon was round the corner. It was all right for them, but she did not know whom to turn to herself. There was no padre she could confess to in the church she attended. She belonged to the Church of England. They had nothing like *Watchtower* and *Awake*, neither had they any system of absolution; they left a guilty person with a nasty conscience. But wait a minute, she told herself, didn't Jesus say to the Pharisees that one should give unto Caesar what was Caesar's and to God what was His? Well, that was what they were doing. She could quote the Holy book to support it. There was nothing to worry about.

The whole family turned out to wish Francis a safe journey at the airport at Ikeja. When husbands left their wives for the UK the wives were all supposed to cry from love. Adah prayed to God the night before to send enough tears to impress her parents-in-law. Those tears of hers had a way of coming down at the wrong time. She wanted them to flow at the airport so that when Francis became an élite he would remember that poor Adah wept for him even when he was a nobody. Well, those tears did come, but at the wrong time. She watched Francis bid everybody good-bye, dry-eyed. All his sisters were like that Alice in Lewis Carroll's fantasy, weeping away like mad. He would remember them when he came back an élite, with strings and strings of qualifications. He will forget me and my child, and the other one I'm going to have in three weeks' time, Adah thought as she stood there, away from the clan, just like an outcast. Francis was disappointed and showed it, but he gave her a pat on the shoulder. Poor Adah, her heart ached for the departure of the only human being she was just beginning to understand, just learning to care for. Maybe the separation was too early in their marriage, she did not know. But what she did know was that there was this ache inside her heart, too heavy for tears, too heavy for words She simply stared at them all.

Everybody's name was being called, and all the passengers stood one at a time, at the plane's door, waved their final good-bye to their folks and then disappeared into the bowels of the whale-like monster they called the aeroplane. Adah had never seen an aeroplane at such close range. Why, they were bigger than buses! she thought. The air hostess was smiling unnaturally and waving two hands instead of one like everybody else. Why was that? Adah wondered. Then the door was cruelly slammed shut. The slamming of that door, the finality of it all, reminded her of something she had seen before. She had seen it all before, this cruel finality. The other person who was shut away from her like that never came back. Where did it happen before? She searched her memory as she stood in that scorching Nigerian sun. Then her mother-in-law moved towards her. Adah did not know what it was that drew that woman towards her in that burning sun. She touched Adah's unfeeling arm, and said in a choked voice: 'It looks like a coffin.' Adah turned round, saw her, and started to howl.

It all came back to her now. It was Pa who was nailed down into the bowels of a smaller whale, because he was going to be the only inhabitant of that one. This one was bigger, but it had the same aura of finality. 'Please God it won't happen again. He is going to arrive there safely. Please God, let nothing bad happen to him,' she cried.

The relatives wiped their eyes and stared at Adah. What was the matter with her? Wives cried in the presence of their departing husbands, not when they had gone and could not see the tears! No one said anything. After all, she was going to provide the cash, so she was allowed a little eccentricity. The fact that someone so young could earn so much as Adah was enough to drive her to extremities, they said.

Francis wrote from Barcelona and then from London. 'You did not cry for me,' he accused Adah in his letters. 'You were very happy to see me go, were you not? Was that why you did not wish to appear in my send-off photograph? You did not care for me.'

Now, with what type of soap was Adah to wash herself clean of this dirty accusation? How was she to write to Francis and say, 'I cried for you. No, I even howled like a mad Zulu woman at the airport because the door of the plane reminded me of my Pa's coffin'? He would think she was mad. So Adah decided against it. She simply let sleeping

34

dogs lie. She sent him money regularly, bore him another child, this time a son, went back to work twelve days afterwards, having had only three weeks' annual leave. There was no provision for maternity benefit at the American Consulate then. But the staff had a big party for her, all American, all very rich and very nice. They knew what Adah was going through, but they were diplomats, not missionaries or social workers.

A few months afterwards Francis sent his wife and parents the results of his Part I examination. He had passed. So, for Adah, it was time to act, or she would never go to the land of her dreams.

She was so happy about Francis's success that she babbled about it to everybody. She was not too surprised about this early success, considering that he had taken this exam four times in Lagos before going to the UK. There was still the second and third parts and, the way Adah calculated it, Francis would stay another four or even five years. In one of his letters, he even mentioned his wanting to be articled. That would take five years at least. What was she supposed to do in the meantime? She wrote and asked Francis this, and was shocked to read from him that he would like her to come, but from her behaviour at the airport he was sure she did not care. Well, that was all she needed.

She went to Francis's mother, appealed to her to look at all the women who had been to England, pointing out the fact that they all drove their own cars.

'Think of it, Ma – Francis in his big American car and I in my small one, coming to visit you and Pa when you retire. You'll be the envy of all your friends. Mind you, in England I'll work and still send you money. All you have to do is to ask, and then you'll get whatever you want. All the girls will go to secondary school. I've almost finished reading for librarianship. All I have to do is to work, look after Francis and attend classes in the evening. And when I come back, I shall earn more than double what I'm earning now.'

Adah won over her mother-in-law. If going to England meant her earning more than she was earning now, and riding a car as well, then she was all for it. Pa was still doubtful. He had suffered from unemployment when he was a

35

young man and knew that the type of job Adah had then did not grow on trees.

'My going to England would be regarded as leave without pay.'

That softened Pa.

The next problem was the children. Her mother-in-law sensed that if Adah took her two babies, she might never send the money she promised. Adah had a good solution for that. She was very fond of jewellery and had invested a small part of her income in this. She had several necklaces for her little girl and herself. She gave them all to her mother-in-law.

'You take them; in England we shan't need them. And when I come back, I shan't be wearing gold any more,' Adah boasted with a faked smile on her face, whilst her heart sent her mother-in-law to her Maker. She never asked Adah what she would be wearing when she came back from England. Diamonds maybe. Mother-in-law was shocked all right and, before she could recover, Adah had had her kids immunized and paid for a first-class passage by boat for the three of them. She was completely deaf to the warnings that she was paying over two hundred pounds more than was necessary for their passage to England. She was told to wait another six months and she would get cheaper accommodation in the cabin-class. Six months was too long a time to wait. Mother-in-law would change her mind.

She was still not completely sure that her dream was coming true until she was on the deck of the *Oriel*, Vicky in her arms and Titi holding on to her skirt. It was then she saw her brother, Boy, in a brown African robe that was too big for him, crying and wiping his eyes with a velvet hat. Adah did not cry for the in-laws, and funnily enough they did not cry for her. But all she needed to know was that a member of her own family was there, missing her. Boy was like Pa and Ma moulded all into one, standing there. She cried too, this time not a howl, not an empty show, but tears of real sorrow at the thought of leaving the land of her birth. The land where Pa was buried and where Ma lay, quiet forever. Only she and Boy remained of that life which she had known. It was never going to be the same again. Things were bound to change, for better or for worse, but they wou.d never be the same.

Boy was now all alone. He had to work very hard to keep the family name going. Adah had dropped out of it. She had become an Obi instead of the Ofili she used to be. Boy had resented this, but his presence at the wharf showed that he had accepted the fact that in Africa, and among the Ibos in particular, a girl was little more than a piece of property. Adah had been bought, though on credit, and she would never go back to being an Ofili any more. The tiny hands clutching her blouse were the hands of a big man in the making. Her duty was to them now. From now on her children came first. All she could do for Boy was to make him aware that he had a sister he had every reason to be proud of. She might not come back a millionaire, but she would come back with pride.

Adah wiped her eyes and waved to her brother, the distance between them lengthening so much that he soon became like a small black comma and then he was gone.

There was no time to wallow in self-pity. All around her were wives of diplomats and top white civil servants going home on leave. Life was changing fast. Being there, in that first-class section, seemed to give her a taste of what was to come. God would help Boy as He had helped her. She gave her children to the nurse, and relaxed. It's nice to be treated like an élite, a status they were achieving. Had not Francis passed his first examination in Cost and Works accountancy, were not she and her children on their way to England? She knew she was determined that they would go to English schools and, if possible, English universities.

She remembered what she had told her mother-in-law the very night before. 'We shall only stay a year and six months.' The poor woman had believed her. That was life, she said to herself. Be as cunning as a serpent and as harmless as a dove.

3 A Cold Welcome

There was a sudden burst of excitement on the deck of the ship. Adah could hear it from where she was sitting in her cabin, changing Vicky's napkin. For a moment she stopped what she was doing, straining her ears to make out what the excitement was about, but she could hear nothing coherent. There were voices jabbering loudly, somebody laughing hysterically, and there were sounds of someone running as if chased by demons.

What could it be? wondered Adah, as she hurried through the diaper routine. Perhaps it was a fire, or an accident, or could it be that they were drowning? She knew they would be in Liverpool in a day or two, but what was the rushing for? She was unable to bear the suspense any longer so she quickly slipped a dress on and ran out on to the deck.

She had forgotten that they had passed the Bay of Biscay, she had forgotten that they were now in Europe and that it was March. The cold wind that blew on her face as she emerged on deck was as heavy and hurtful as a blow from a boxer. She ran back, with her arms folded across her chest, to get more clothes. Then she ran to the ship's nurse. The nurse had a fat face, small eyes and a fat body. She was all smiles when she saw Adah and her eyes were lost in creases.

'Have you seen it?' she burbled. 'Have you seen Liverpool? It's too early and a bit dark, but we are in Liverpool. We've arrived in England!'

Adah opened her eyes wide and closed them again, still shivering. So they had arrived. She had arrived in the United Kingdom. *Pa, I'm in the United Kingdom*, her heart sang to her dead father.

The nurse stared at her for a second, then dashed past her, anxious to spread the good news.

Adah put on the woolies which she bought at Las Palmas. Then she ran out on to the deck.

England gave Adah a cold welcome. The welcome was particularly cold because only a few days previously they had been enjoying bright and cheerful welcomes from ports like Takoradi, Freetown and Las Palmas. If Adah had been Jesus, she would have passed England by. Liverpool was grey, smoky and looked uninhabited by humans. It reminded Adah of the loco-yard where they told her Pa had once worked as a moulder. In fact the architectural designs were the same. But if, as people said, there was plenty of money in England, why then did the natives give their visitors this poor cold welcome? Well, it was too late to moan, it was too late to change her mind. She could not have changed it even if she had wanted to. Her children must have an English education and, for that reason, she was prepared to bear the coldest welcome, even if it came from the land of her dreams. She was a little bit disappointed, but she told herself not to worry. If people like Lawyer Nweze and others could survive it, so could she.

The Francis that came to meet them was a new Francis. There was something very, very different about him. Adah was stunned when he kissed her in public, with everybody looking. Oh, my God, she thought; if her mother-in-law could see them, she would go and make sacrifices to Oboshi for forgiveness. Francis was delighted with Vicky.

'Just my image, I can now die in peace!'

'What do you mean, die in peace?' Adah challenged.

Francis laughed. 'In England, people make jokes of everything, even things as serious as death. People still laugh about them.'

'Yes?' Adah was beginning to be scared. She looked round her wildly.

There were hundreds of people rushing around clutching their luggage, and pulling their children, but it was not as noisy as it would have been had they been in Lagos. The whites she saw did not look like people who could make jokes about things like death. They looked remote, happy in an aloof way, but determined to keep their distance.

'These people don't look as if they know how to joke. You're lying, Francis. You're making it all up. English people don't joke about death.'

'This separation of ours has made you bold. You've never in your life told me that I was lying before,' Francis accused.

Adah was quietened by the sharpness of his voice. The sharpness seemed to say to her: 'It is allowed for African males to come and get civilized in England, but that privilege has not been extended to females yet.' She would have liked to protest about it from the very beginning, but what was the point of their quarrelling on the very first day of their meeting after such a long separation? It is a sad indication, though, of what was coming, but she prayed that the two of them would be strong enough to accept civilization into their relationship. Because if they did not, their coming would have been a very big mistake.

After the tedious check by the immigration officers, they shivered themselves into the train. It sped on and on for hours. For the first time Adah saw real snow. It all looked so beautiful after the greyness of Liverpool. It was as if there were beautiful white clouds on the ground. She saw the factory where Ovaltine was made. Somehow that factory, standing there isolated, clean and red against the snowy background, lightened her spirit. She was in England at last. She was beginning to feel like Dick Whittington!

Francis had told her in his letter that he had accommodation for them in London. He did not warn Adah what it was like. The shock of it all nearly drove her crazy.

The house was grey with green windows. She could not tell where the house began and where it ended, because it was joined to other houses in the street. She had never seen houses like that before, joined together like that. In Lagos houses were usually completely detached with the yards on both sides, the compound at the back and verandas in front. These ones had none of those things. They were long solid blocks, with doors opening into the street. The windows were arranged in straight rows along the streets. On looking round, Adah noticed that one could tell which windows belonged to which door by the colour the frames were painted.

Most of the houses seemed to have the same curtains for thei.
windows.

'They all look like churches, you know; monasteries,'
Adah remarked.

'They build their houses like that here because land is not
as plentiful as it is in Lagos. I am sure that builders of the
future will start building our houses like that when Nigeria is
fully industrialized. At the moment we can afford to waste
land in building spacious verandas and back yards.'

'We may never be as bad as this. Jammed against each
other.'

Francis did not make any comment. There was no need.
He opened the door into what looked to Adah like a tunnel.
But it was a hall; a hall with flowered walls! It was narrow
and it seemed at first as if there were no windows. Adah
clutched at Titi, and she in turn held her mother in fear.
They climbed stairs upon stairs until they seemed to be
approaching the roof of the house. Then Francis opened
one door and showed them into a room, or a half-room. It
was very small with a single bed at one end and a new
settee which Francis had bought with the money Adah sent
him to buy her a top coat with. The space between the
settee and the bed was just enough for a Formica-topped
table, the type she had had in the kitchen in Lagos.

'Are we going to live here?' she managed to ask.

'Well, I know you will not like it, but this is the best I
can do. You see, accommodation is very short in London,
especially for black people with children. Everybody is coming
to London. The West Indians, the Pakistanis and even the
Indians, so that African students are usually grouped together
with them. We are all blacks, all coloureds, and the only
houses we can get are horrors like these.'

Well, what could she say? She simply stared. She said
nothing even when she learned that the toilet was outside,
four flights of stairs down, in the yard; nor when she learned
that there was no bath and no kitchen. She swallowed it all,
just like a nasty pill.

In the evening, the other tenants returned from the factories
where they worked. They all came to welcome her. Then, to
her horror, she saw that she had to share the house with

41

such Nigerians who called her madam at home; some of them were of the same educational background as her paid servants. She knew she had had a terrible childhood, but still, in Nigeria, class distinctions were beginning to be established. *Oh, Francis*, she wailed inwardly, *how could you have done this to us? After all we have friends who, though they may be living in slums like this, still live apart from this type of people.*

'You could have tried, Francis. Look at your friend, Mr Eke – when he knew that his wife was coming with their daughter, he made sure he moved away from this lot,' she said aloud.

'Sorry, but I was too busy. It's not bad, you can keep to yourself, you don't have to mix with them. You have your children to look after, you don't have to see them!'

'You make it all sound so easy – "I don't have to see them." You forget I have young children, and they will bring me into contact with the neighbours. You should have thought of that before. Have you no shame at all or have you lost your sense of shame in this God-forsaken country? Oh, I wish I had not come. I wish I had been warned. ᵀ wish...'

'Why don't you stop wishing and face reality? It is too late now. We just have to make the best of the situation. I shouldn't start moaning, if I were you.'

'Don't talk to me. I don't want to hear. You could have got better accommodation if you had really tried. But you didn't try hard enough,' Adah yelled.

Francis's temper snapped. He lifted his hand as if to slap her, but thought better of it. There would be plenty of time for that, if Adah was going to start telling him what to do. This scared Adah a little. He would not have dreamt of hitting her at home because his mother and father would not have allowed it. To them, Adah was like the goose that laid the golden eggs. It seemed that in England, Francis didn't care whether she laid the golden egg or not. He was free at last from his parents, he was free to do what he liked, and not even hundreds of Adahs were going to curtail that new freedom. The ugly glare he gave Adah made that clear.

Then he spat out in anger: 'You must know, my dear young *lady*, that in Lagos you may be a million publicity officers for the Americans; you may be earning a million pounds a day; you may have hundreds of servants: you may be living like an élite, but the day you land in England, you are a second-class citizen. So you can't discriminate against your own people, because we are all second-class.'

He stopped to see the effect of his warning. He was happy to see that it had made an impression. Adah sat crumpled on the edge of the new settee, just like the dying Ayesha in Rider Haggard's *She*.

Francis went on, enjoying the rhythm of his voice. That man should have been an actor, Adah thought.

He laughed. A joyless sort of laugh, dry and empty. 'I remember at one of your Old Girls' Association meetings where that white lady . . . yes, I remember, she was from Oxford, wasn't she? – I remember her telling you all that young women with your background should never in all your lives talk to bus conductors. Well, my darling, in England the middle-class black is the one that is lucky enough to get the post of bus conductor. So you'd better start respecting them.'

At first Adah thought Francis hated her. This was his first opportunity of showing her what he was really like. Had she made a mistake in rushing into this marriage? But she had needed a home. And the immigration authorities were making it very difcult for single girls to come to England. You were allowed only as long as you were coming to join a husband who was already there. It was very bad, sad in fact. But even if she had nothing to thank Francis for, she could still thank him for making it possible for her to come to England, for giving her her own children, because she had never really had anything of her own before.

They made it up that night, forgetting, in their intense disappointment and loneliness which was fast descending upon them like a gloomy cloud, that they were not supposed to have more children for some time. Adah did remember in the confusion that her nickname at home was 'Touch not'. But how could she protest to a man who was past reasoning? The whole process was an attack, as savage as that of any animal.

At the end of it all, Francis gasped and said, 'Tomorrow

you are going to see a doctor. I want them to see this frigidity. I am not going to have it.'

When, days later, Adah discovered what frigidity meant, she realized that Francis had become sophisticated in many things. She kept all this to herself, though. There was no point in arguing with Francis; he was as remote as the English people Adah had seen at Liverpool. And the house where they now lived was a place in which one could not have a good family ding-dong in peace.

What worried her most was the description 'second-class'. Francis had become so conditioned by this phrase that he was not only living up to it but enjoying it, too. He kept pressing Adah to get a job in a shirt factory. Adah refused. Working in a factory was the last thing she would do. After all, she had several 'O' and 'A' levels and she had part of the British Library Association Professional Certificate, to say nothing of experience. Why should she go and work with her neighbours who were just learning to join their letters together instead of printing them? Some of them could not even speak any English even though it was becoming a colloquial language for most Ibos. To cap it all, these people were Yorubas, the type of illiterate Yoruba who would take joy in belittling anything Ibo. But Francis mixed with them very well, and they were pushing him to force her to take the type of job considered suitable for housewives, especially black housewives.

This was all too much for Adah, and she recoiled into her shell, telling it all, as the Protestant hymn books says, 'to God in prayers'.

But, as usual, God had a funny way of answering people's prayers. An envelope arrived one morning telling her that she had been accepted as a senior library assistant at North Finchley Library subject to certain conditions. She was so happy about this that she ran into the back yard where she hung out the babies' nappies and started to whirl round and round in a kind of Ibo dance. She was forced to stop suddenly because she was dizzy. She was unwell. She was, in fact, feeling sick.

Then she remembered that first night. Oh, God help her, what was she going to do? Tell Francis in his present mood?

He would kill her. He had started accusing her of all sorts of things. He had told her that he married her in the first place because she could work harder than most girls of her age and because she was orphaned very early in life. But since she had arrived in England, she had grown too proud to work.

The news of the new job would have cheered him up, but not if it was coupled with the knowledge that another child was on the way when Titi was barely two and Vicky nine months old; not when the two children were not yet out of nappies? Oh, God, what was she going to do? Francis would say she had invented the pregnancy to avoid work. Had he not taken her to see a female gynaecologist the very next day because, as he said, no marriage succeeds without a good sex life? As far as he was concerned, marriage was sex and lots of it, nothing more. The doctor was very sympathetic towards Adah and guessed that she was frightened of another child. She was sent home equipped with all sorts of gadgets to prevent a baby that was already sitting there prettily. Oh, yes, Bubu was determined to come into the world, and nobody was able to stop him even though he chose a very unorthodox way of doing so, nine months later. Meanwhile his mother went through hell.

Adah felt very ill, but kept it quiet. Francis was dissatisfied and started shopping around outside for willing women. Adah was quite happy about this; she even encouraged him. At least she would have some peaceful nights.

As she expected, Francis blamed her for the baby, and was sure she would lose the job because there was to be a medical examination. Adah was scared about this, but she was determined to get that job.

She put on her best skirt and blouse, the set she had bought from St Michael's in Lagos. She had not been able to buy any clothes since she arrived in England as all the money she had brought with her went on food. Francis would not work as he was studying and he said this would interfere with his progress. Well, she put on this outfit, feeling great. She had not really dressed up for a very long time. Apart from making her feel good, the skirt and blouse covered the gentle bulge that was already forming. Being the third child, it showed early.

She stopped panicking when she saw that the doctor was a man, and an old man at that. There was a woman sitting by him, though, a scribe or something, for she held a pen and paper and sat on a chair, as stiff as dry twigs. Adah ignored the latter and set to work on the old doctor. She beamed at him, charmed him and even wanted to flirt with him. In short, the doctor got carried away and forgot to look at Adah's belly-button, even though she was stripped to the waist.

She got the job. Only God Almighty knew what happened to the poor doctor, especially as it was clear from the first month that she was pregnant and she enquired about maternity leave. Adah was sorry for him, but what could she have done? If she had not got that job her marriage would have broken up, and that would have been very difficult because she did not yet know her way about. The fact that she was still laying the golden eggs stopped Francis from walking out on her. As before, her pay bound him to her but the difference was that she now knew it.

She had had to travel all the way from Lagos to London to find that out, and to discover another very weak point: she cared for Francis, she wanted him to make good, she hated to disappoint him. So, sorry though she was for making a fool of an old doctor, this was just one of those cases where honesty would not have been the best policy.

4 The Daily Minders

Adah started work on the first of June. It was almost three months since she arrived in the United Kingdom. She was so proud of her job and so happy on this particular June morning that she found beauty in everything. She saw beauty on the faces of her fellow passengers and heard beautiful sounds from the churning groans of the speeding underground train.

Spring had come very late that year, because it had been a long and bitter winter, and although it was June, the freshness in the air was like that of the first day of April.

At Finchley Central, the train emerged from its underground tunnel into the open air like a snake from its hole. Adah let down the window and breathed in the cool, pure, watery air. It had rained the night before and there was wetness everywhere.

She saw the back gardens of many, many houses, gardens with flowers of many varieties growing in profusion: lupins and peonies, delphiniums, sweet peas and columbines. The wonderful glow of alyssum on the verges of many garden paths gave a tidy edge to the carpet of green grass which seemed to cover the ground. The trees had burst into green, ceasing to look like the naked, dried-up, juiceless old women they had reminded Adah of when she first landed in England.

Now, everything was young, clean, moist and full of juice.

At the library, she was quickly taken under the wing of the chief librarian. She was a Czech, explosive in her welcome and very, very friendly. Mrs Konrad was a wide lady, with wide hips, a wide waist, and a face like a flattened O. She had fine lines around her eyes, and these lines deepened when she smiled, which was most of the time. Even her smiles were wide, displaying her creamy, even teeth.

She seemed to have little time for make-up. Her brown hair was cropped, just like a man's used to be before the arrival of Jesus fashion. She left a handful of bulbous curls at the back of her head and another at the front; the latter had a funny way of collapsing on to her forehead, and she was forever pushing them back into their rightful place. The curls at the back stayed there unperturbed, even when Mrs Konrad shook with laughter.

Her skirts were always gathered and home-made. She wore woollen gathered ones in winter and cotton gathered ones in summer. She was untouched by any passing fashion. Come tight skirts, wide skirts, come midis, minis, maxis, Mrs Konrad aways wore her gathered skirts. This, together with unusually tight blouses, gave her the look of an overblown ballet dancer.

The other girls were assistants, very young with long, skinny legs; most of them seemed to be all legs to Adah. Unlike their superior, they were all fashion-conscious. They made Adah feel out of place, so she never really became too familiar with them. They made her feel inferior somehow, always talking of boy-friends and clothes. Adah would have liked to join in, for she was the same age, but she knew that if she opened her mouth she would sound bitter. She would have told them that marriage was not a bed of roses but a tunnel of thorns, fire and hot nails. Oh, yes, she would have told them all sorts of things. But why, she asked herself, must she spoil other people's dreams? So she preferred to listen and smile noncommittally.

Soon she settled down to work. She hardly ever sat down, and this was purgatorial to her feet. Only God knew what the people of North Finchley did with all the books they borrowed. The queue sometimes stretched so far that some people had to stand outside, waiting, just to borrow books. This was a big contrast to the library she had worked in before. In the consulate, they had to bribe people to make them read fiction. They were only keen on reading text-books in order to raise their status economically. No one bothered with fiction. But in North Finchley, the number of fiction readers was so staggering that Adah decided to emulate them. She, too, started to read the works of many contemporary novelists, and that helped her a great deal culturally.

In her new job, she had to be very fast in filing books, in filing tickets, in making out readers' tickets, in tracing lost ones. And all the time she was forever saying 'Thank you'; 'Thank you' when she accepted the returned books, 'Thank you' when she gave the tickets back, 'Thank you' when she handed over new books. In fact, working at the North Finchley Library was more of a 'Thank you, thank you' job than anything else. All in all, Adah was happy she'd got a first-class job; she was happy that her colleagues at work liked her, she was happy that she was enjoying her work.

It was all right for her, being a first-class citizen for the part of the day when she worked in a clean, centrally-heated library, but what about her children? Who was going to look after them? Since it was nearing the end of the summer term, Francis did agree to look after them temporarily. While it was still news that she had got herself employed in a library, doing a first-class citizen's job, Francis was prepared to look after their children, but soon her job was no longer news. Everybody accepted it with a sniff.

'Who is going to look after your children for you?' Francis asked one day when he was tucking the babies into their settee bed. 'I can't go on doing it; you'll have to look for someone. I can't go on looking after your children for you.'

Adah spun round, aghast. She was not really surprised that Francis said this, she had known it was coming; but what she hadn't realized was the resentment over the children which was accumulating in Francis. She could sense the suppressed anger when he referred to them as 'her' children, not 'theirs'. In Nigeria, when children were good, they were the father's, they took after him, but when they were bad, they were the mother's, taking after her and her old mother. Adah was frightened.

She could feel their neighbours speaking through Francis. Their landlord and landlady were in their late thirties. They had been married for ten years or more, but the wife had had no children. They had resented Francis's idea of bringing his children to England in the first place. They had warned him that it was going to be difficult for them, but left him alone when he told them that Adah had already paid for their fare. They consoled themselves with the fact that, after all, the children would not stay with their parents at Ashdown Street. They would have to be fostered. Most Nigerians with children sent their children away to foster-parents. No sane couple would dream of keeping their children with them. So rampant was the idea of foster-parents that African housewives in England came to regard the foster-mother as the mother of their children.

They say that in England Nigerian children have two sets of mothers – the natal mother, and the social mother. As soon as a Nigerian housewife in England realized that she was expecting a child, instead of shopping for prams, and knitting little bootees, she would advertise for a foster-mother. No one cared whether a woman was suitable or not, no one wanted to know whether the house was clean or not; all they wanted to be sure of was that the foster-mother was white. The concept of 'whiteness' could cover a multitude of sins.

This was all right for the Nigerian wife who, for the first time, was tasting the real freedom of being a wife. She was free from the hindering influences of her kith and kin, she was free to work and earn money. Any type of work would do: cleaning, packing goods in a factory, being a bus conductor; all sorts of things. The money she thus earned went partly to the foster-mother, and the rest was blown on colourful outfits from some big department store.

Most Nigerian wives would say that they had to send their children away because they lacked suitable accommodation for them, and there was a great deal of truth in this. But what they would not admit was that most of them were brought up in situations, far, far different from the ones in which they found themselves in England. At home in Nigeria, all a mother had to do for a baby was wash and feed him and, if he was fidgety, strap him on to her back and carry on with her work while that baby slept. But in England she had to wash piles and piles of nappies, wheel the child round for sunshine during the day, attend to his feeds as regularly as if one were serving a master, talk to the child, even if he was only a day old! Oh, yes, in England, looking

50

do would be to convince her that, at the age of sixteen, she was too young to keep her baby. But Janet wanted her baby.

This story awakened the communal African spirit in Babalola. It never occurred to him that he was doing anything illegal, taking in a sixteen-year-old girl. On the contrary, Babalola started to entertain his few remaining friends with Janet. It never occurred to him that he might fall in love with her, that he might want to protect her, to make her his wife; at that time, Janet was being offered to any black man who wanted to know how a white woman looked undressed. Most of Adah's neighbours had had their sexual adventures with Janet. But soon all that changed.

Babalola realized that Janet could get dole money for herself and her child, enough to pay the rent. Janet, not knowing where else to go and also, like Adah, coming to terms with Babalola's weaknesses, complied. Soon Babalola started to monopolize Janet.

'You are not thinking of going straight with that thing you picked up at a kiosk?' his friends asked, astonished.

Babalola said nothing, but gave orders to Janet to stop being liberal with his friends any more. Janet, feeling wanted at last, glowed. Soon after her first baby, she became pregnant with her second, Babalola's.

It was at this time that Adah arrived. They became friends straight away. Adah found Janet very intelligent and realized that the rumours about her sleeping around were not true. She only wanted a roof over her head so that she could bring up her little boy, Tony. He was then a noisy eighteen-month-old baby who was a good playmate for Titi.

Adah told Janet about her troubles and Janet confided in Adah. She suggested that Adah should look for a daily-minder for her children until the nursery had vacancies for them. Even Babalola was willing to help – by now he had become unpopular with his friends because he refused to hand his 'fish and chips' girl around. The search was really depressing. It reached a point where Adah had started knocking on door after door. Things got even worse for her when Francis failed his summer examinations. He blamed it all on her. If she had not brought her children and saddled him with

after babies was in itself a full-time job. This was difficult for a Nigerian wife to cope with, especially when she realized that she could no longer count on the help the extended family usually gave in such situations. So most Nigerian children born to the so-called 'students' were condemned to be fostered away.

Everybody expected Adah to do the same. It came as a big surprise, therefore, when they realized that she was not making any attempt to look for a foster-mother. And now Francis told her that he was not going to look after her children for her any more.

Things were difficult for Francis, too. He had never in all his life been allowed to make his own mistakes because he had never made his own decisions. He had always consulted his mother, his father and his brothers. In England he had to make do with his Nigerian neighbours. Adah guessed that they had laughed at him behind her back when she was at work. So she took a deep breath before replying.

'I thought we decided that you were to look after them until we got a nursery place . . . I thought . . .'

'You mean you decided; you thought it all out, and then you tell me what I'm going to do. Everybody laughs at us in this place. No African child lives with his parents. It is not convenient; it is not possible. There is no accommodation for it. Moreover, they won't learn good English. They are much, much better off with an English woman.'

'But you forget, Francis, that when we were young, we spoke Yoruba flawlessly, even though we are Ibos. We picked the language up at school and at play. That shouldn't be difficult. Our English, yours and mine, is not all that bad,' Adah explained in her gentlest voice, aware all the time that she was not only arguing with Francis, but with all the other tenants in Ashdown Street.

He considered this for a while, and then replied: 'But they have no friends to play with.'

'But they will have, when they start at the nursery. I am sure they will.'

Adah was hoping for the impossible. It would be easier for a loaded camel to go through the eye of a sewing needle than for a child with two parents to get a nursery place. The waiting list was a mile long.

Then the landlord started his intimidation. The children must leave the house. He even took it upon himself to advertise for a foster-mother for them. Luckily, no one offered to take 'two black children, boy and girl, aged nine months and two years respectively'. The landlady sensed that Adah did not like it and left her alone.

But the men persisted. Another couple, the Ojos, who had left their four children behind, advised Adah to send hers back to Nigeria. Everybody talked and speculated. The trouble was that Adah was like a peacock, who kept wanting to win all the time. Only first-class citizens lived with their children, not the blacks.

They were right, in a way. The housing conditions were so bad that for days she didn't see Francis at all. As soon as she arrived home from work he would disappear for fresh air. The children had no amusements and their parents would not let them out for fear they would break their necks on the steep stairs. They were hushed and bullied into silence so that the landlord and his wife should not be disturbed. When it rained, which was often, the nappies were dried in the same room. The second-hand heater they used always smoked. The Obis lived not as human beings at all, but like animals.

To cap it all, after the day's work, Adah did not have sufficient space to sleep in. Francis was getting very fat, and their single bed was not big enough for him, let alone the pregnant Adah. So, usually, when she was not needed by her husband, she would squeeze in on the settee with her babies.

At about this time she met and became friendly with a Cockney girl called Janet.

Janet was Mr Babalola's wife. Her story was not only remarkable, but startling as well.

Mr Babalola had come to England, just like Francis and Adah, to study. But, unlike Adah and Francis, he had been single, and had a Northern Nigerian Scholarship. This meant that he had more money to spend, because the Northerners, unlike the over-educated Southerners, would do anything to encourage the men to really get educated so that they could come home and obtain the jobs in the North which were

then going to the Southerners. Mr Babalola was, theref[ore] very rich student.

Rumour had it that he had a glossy flat and was al[ways] entertaining. This was no surprise to anyone who knew [the] Northerners. They liked to spend their money, to really en[joy] what they had, and to them what they had was theirs o[nly] today, not tomorrow or the day after. Allah would take ca[re] of the future. That was certainly Babalola's philosophy o[f] life.

For some reason, however, the money for Mr Babalola stopped coming, no one knew why. One thing was sure, he was not doing any studying, though he had come originally to read journalism. Word went round that he was getting poor. He could not maintain his old level of entertainment, so his friends of the happier days took to their heels. They stopped coming, and Babalola moved to a much more modest area – Ashdown Street in Kentish Town.

It was at this time, when his funds were running low and he was desperately trying to convince his government that, given another opportunity, he would do well, that he met Janet.

He was waiting impatiently at a telephone kiosk to make a call to one of his now elusive friends. He waited for what seemed ages, but the young woman already in the kiosk seemed to clutch at the receiver for hours. Many others came, got tired of waiting and left, grumbling. But Babalola waited. He was going to make his call, even if it took him all day. It started to drizzle and he was getting soaked to the skin, so he banged on the kiosk door, and shook his fist at the girl to frighten her. Then he looked closer, and saw that the girl was not phoning anybody, she was asleep, standing up.

Babalola's first reaction was fear. Was she dead, he wondered? Then he banged harder and the girl woke. He was so sorry for her that he took her home.

Janet was pregnant. The father of her baby was a nameless West Indian. Her stepfather would not take her in unless she promised to give the child away. Her mother had died a year before, leaving her stepfather seven young children to look after. Janet was the oldest, so she had been turned out of the house. She would not go to any social worker; all he would

them, if she had allowed them to be fostered, if she had not become pregnant so soon after her arrival, he would have passed.

Francis forgot that it had taken him five attempts to pass the first part, that he did not attend any lectures because he felt he could do better on his own, that he was always reluctant to get up early enough in the mornings.

Luckily for Adah, Babalola heard of Trudy. She had two children of her own and agreed to look after Adah's two as well. Francis praised Trudy to the skies. She was clean, well dressed and very friendly. Adah had not seen her yet, because she usually worked late in the library, coming home at eight o'clock most evenings.

She would dress the children, and Francis wheeled them to Trudy's, which was just a block away, and collected them at six, after Trudy had washed them and given them tea. That, at least, was the arrangement.

After a few weeks, Adah noticed that Titi stopped talking altogether. This surprised Adah because Titi was a real chatterbox. She wondered what was happening and decided to take the children to Trudy herself. After all, she had carried them for nine months, not Francis. Francis was happy about this because he claimed that his friends laughed at him when they saw him with his children in a pushchair.

What struck Adah first was the fact that Trudy's milkman delivered only two pints every morning even though she was given Adah's children's milk coupon. But Trudy told her that Adah's children took three pints a day and that her milkman delivered not the two Adah saw, but five pints every day.

Adah said nothing, but started giving her children cereal before leaving for work. This meant extra work, but she would do all she could to bring Titi back to her old self again.

Still uneasy, she started paying Trudy visits on her half-days. She did not like what she saw. Trudy's house, like all the houses in that area, was a slum. A house that had been condemned ages ago. The back yard was filled with rubbish, broken furniture, and very near an uncovered dustbin was the toilet, the old type of toilet with faulty plumbing, smelly and damp.

On the first day that Adah went, she saw Trudy's two little girls playing in the front garden. They both had red slacks and blue pullovers. Their long brown hair was tied with well-pressed red ribbons. They were laughing and looked very happy. They swung something in the air and Adah realized that Trudy's girls were playing with the spades and buckets that she had bought for her own children. Her heart burned with anger, but she told herself to stop behaving like the little Ibo tigress. After all, she had not stayed five good years at the Methodist Girls' High School for nothing. At least she had been taught to tame her emotions. Maybe her children were having a nap or something.

She walked in and entered the sitting-room. She saw Trudy, a plump woman with too much make-up. Her lips were scarlet and so were her nails. The colour of her hair was too black to be natural. Maybe it was originally brown like those of her little girls; but the jet black dye gave her whole personality a sort of vulgarity. She was laughing loudly at a joke she was sharing with a man who was holding her at a funny angle. Adah closed her eyes. The laughter stopped abruptly when they noticed her.

'Why aren't you at work?' Trudy gasped.

'I was going to the clinic at Malden Road, so I thought I'd look in and see how you were getting on with Titi and Vicky.'

There was a pause, during which Adah could hear her heartbeat racing. She was finding it more and more difficult to control her temper. She remembered her mother. Ma would have torn the fatty tissues of this woman into shreds if she had been in this situation. Well, she was not Ma, but she was Ma's daughter, and, come what may, she was still an Ibo. She screamed.

'Where are my children? You pro –' She stopped herself. She was about to call Trudy a prostitute, but was not sure whether the man watching them, with his flies open, was her husband or not. The man quickly excused himself though, and Adah blamed herself for not completing her sentence. The man was not Trudy's husband. He was a lover; a customer or a boy-friend, or maybe a mixture of both. Adah did not care. She wanted to see her children.

Trudy pointed towards the door. Adah's eyes followed the pointing finger to the back yard. Yes, Adah could hear the faint voice of Vicky, babbling something in his own special language. She ran out and saw her children. She stood there, her knees shaking and burst into tears.

Vicky was busy pulling rubbish out of the bin and Titi was washing her hands and face with the water leaking from the toilet. When they saw her, they ran to her, and Adah noticed that Vicky had no nappy on.

'They won't talk to us. The other day I gave an ice-cream to Titi, and she did not know what to do with it. They wet themselves all the time.' Trudy went on and on like a woman possessed, talking non-stop.

Adah bundled the children into their push-chair and took them to the children's officer at Malden Road. After all, Trudy was a registered baby-minder, whatever that was supposed to mean.

The children's officer tut-tutted a great deal. Adah was given a cup of tea and told not to worry too much. After all, the children were all right, weren't they?

While they were still talking, Trudy arrived in floods of tears. She protested that she had only allowed them into the back yard that day because she had a stinking visitor who would not go. Had Adah not seen him? He wouldn't leave her alone. Of course the children had wandered into the back yard. She wouldn't have the heart to put a dog there, to say nothing of little 'angels' like Adah's kids. She was a registered daily-minder. Registered by the Borough of Camden. If her standards had been low, she would not have been registered in the first place. Adah should ask Miss Stirling.

Miss Stirling was the children's officer. She wore a red dress and rimless spectacles, the type academics in old photographs usually wore. She blinked a great deal. She was blinking now, as her name was mentioned. But she could not get a word in, Trudy was making all the running.

As for Adah, she listened to Trudy destroying forever one of the myths she had been brought up to believe: that the white man never lied. She had grown up among white missionaries who were dedicated to their work, she had then worked among American diplomats who were working for their country in Nigeria, and since she came to England the only other whites she had actually mixed with were the girls in the library and Janet. She had never met the like of Trudy before. In fact she could not believe her ears; she just gaped in astonishment.

Trudy even went as far as to tell the children's officer that Adah's kids drank five pints of milk a day. She loved the children, she said, and to prove it she made a grab at Titi, but the child recoiled, protesting wildly.

Trudy was reprimanded and she promised to mend her ways. She would never let the children out of her sight. Six pounds a week was not easy to come by especially for a woman who stayed at home all day.

She babbled all the way home, telling Adah her whole life history and the history of her parents and her grandparents. But Adah could not stop thinking about her discovery that the whites were just as fallible as everyone else. There were bad whites and good whites, just as there were bad blacks and good blacks! Why, then, did they claim to be superior?

From that day on she took everything Trudy said with a pinch of salt. Francis told her not to worry. Even if the children were left in the back yard, he was sure it must have been clean before the kids messed it up. Instead he told Titi and Vicky to be good children and never, never go near the rubbish dump again because dustbins were dirty. The babies just stared at him. Then he told Titi that if she did not keep herself dry, he would beat her with his belt.

But how was Titi to obey an order that she did not understand? In Nigeria and on the boat, she was a noisy toddler, talking and singing in Yoruba like all her little friends. Adah was teaching her English sentences, and sometimes read her nursery rhymes, of which 'Baa baa, black sheep' was her favourite. But now she simply refused to talk. Adah worried so much about it and spoke to God about it in her prayers.

Then one day a friend and classmate of hers came to visit them. Not having anything to give her, Adah decided to make her a bowl of custard. When her back was turned, the friend started to tease Titi in Yoruba, encouraging her to talk. Tired of Titi's silence, Adah's friend snapped at Titi: 'Have you lost or sold your tongue? You used to talk to me in Nigeria? Why don't you talk to me now?'

Then Titi, the poor thing, snapped back in Yoruba: 'Don't talk to me. My dad will cane me with the belt if I speak in Yoruba. And I don't know much English. Don't talk to me.'

Adah was so startled that she spilled the hot custard she was making. So that was it! Francis wanted their daughter to start speaking only in English.

This was due to the fact that Nigeria was ruled for so long a time by the English. An intelligent man was judged by the way he spoke English. But it did not matter whether the English could speak the languages of the people they ruled. This convention had a terrible effect on little Titi. She later overcame her difficulty in speaking, but she was well over six years old before she mastered any language sufficiently well to be able to converse intelligently. That early confusion retarded her verbal development a great deal. But, thank God, it did not land her in one of those special schools for backward children!

After that revelation, Adah started nagging Miss Stirling to find a nursery place for her children. But, as every young mother who tried to place her child in a nursery could testify, there was no place for the children.

She had to make do with Trudy, aware all the time that the kids still played in the back yard and that Vicky's nappies were never used, but soaked in water so that they looked used.

She prayed to God about it, and hoped nothing horrid would happen to the kids. God was either tired of answering her prayers, or wanted to teach Adah a lesson. For something horrid did happen, not to Titi, but to Vicky.

5 An Expensive Lesson

One beautiful morning in July, Adah woke up very tired. There were many possible reasons that could have accounted for her fatigue: their living conditions, cramped together in one half-room; her constant worry about the way Vicky and Titi were being treated; her pregnancy. To cap it all, she and Francis communicated only in monosyllables, and then only when the conversation was very necessary.

She started to lose faith in herself. Had her dream of coming to the United Kingdom been right after all, or was she simply an empty dreamer? Put Francis had agreed to it in the first place. Where had she gone wrong? She wished the Presence was still with her to give her a clue but it seemed to have deserted her when she landed in England. Was the Presence her instinct? It had been very active in Nigeria. Was that because in Nigeria she was nearer to Mother Nature? She only wished somebody would tell her where she had gone wrong.

With this heaviness which was like the heavy load of Christian in *The Pilgrim's Progress*, she got up reluctantly. She looked for a minute or two at her husband snoring away, his hairy chest going up and down like troubled waves. She felt like shaking him to tell him how tired she was feeling, and how reluctant she was to leave the house and the children that day but she knew that he would not listen in the first place, and even if he listened, he would dismiss her feelings as mere superstition, just like Caesar dismissed his wife's dream about the Ides of March.

She got herself dressed, washed the children and gave them breakfast. The clatter of the plates and Vicky's crying woke Francis eventually.

'What's all this noise about so early in the morning? Can't

I even have an eight hours' sleep in peace?' Francis demanded angrily.

'Vicky won't have his Rice Krispies. I don't know what's the matter with him this morning. He isn't hot or anything, just raging with temper at nothing,' Adah explained.

Francis looked at his son for a while. Vicky stood in the middle of the room with his mouth pouting in determined anger, and his bib dripping with milk. Francis sighed and was on the verge of turning over to face the other side of the bed when Adah said:

'I feel so heavy this morning, and have no appetite either. Could you please take the children to Trudy for me? I'm late as it is.'

'Oh, God,' groaned her husband.

'Will you take them for me?' Adah pleaded.

'Have I any choice?' Francis wanted to know.

Such questions did not need answers, Adah decided within herself, but she was annoyed nonetheless. Could Francis not have asked her how she was feeling or something? Would that be too much to ask? she wondered. She told herself to stop being over-romantic and soft. No husband would have time to ask his pregnant wife how she was feeling so early in the morning. That only happened in *True Stories* and *True Romances*, not in real life, particularly not with Francis for that matter. But despite the hard talking to herself, she still yearned to be loved, to feel really married, to be cared for. She was beginning to understand why some young wives went to the extent of being unfaithful, just to make themselves feel human, just to find another human being who would listen to their voices, who would tell them that it was going to be all right.

Francis was only good at giving her children, nothing else. She felt vengeful. She left the breakfast things uncleared, did not change Vicky's dripping bib, did not wipe the milky mouth; she simply pulled out her bag from the jumble of children's clothes and walked to the door, about to leave.

Then Vicky, seeing his mother was leaving him, started to cry. In his hurry to grab her skirt, he tipped more milk on to the carpetless floor. Adah smiled inwardly. Francis was going to have a busy day.

She picked Vicky up, cooed to him reassuringly and kissed him. But Vicky would not let her go. He held on to her tightly. That was odd, thought Adah. Vicky was a contented, fat baby, who normally just said 'bye-bye' to Adah most mornings. But not today. Adah sat down again and cuddled him, sang to him, and then the 'bye-bye' came. A tearful one, a reluctant one. He walked to the door, this time clutching at a teaspoon, still wearing the dripping bib. As for Titi, she was past caring. She seemed scarcely aware of all the goings-on around her. She seemed to have resigned herself to the inevitability of it all. She seemed to tell her little self that her crying would not change anything and she must accept things as they were.

Adah's pay at work was just enough to pay the rent, pay for Francis's course, his examination fees, buy his books and pay Trudy. They had little left after this, and so it was impossible for Adah to have lunch at work. She usually took a boiled egg with her, instead of having it in the mornings for breakfast. But sometimes she got bored with having just a boiled egg and the coffee provided in the library and she ate nothing. On those occasions, she felt that type of hunger which she thought she had outgrown. The hunger that held the two sides of one's stomach and squeezed them so tightly that the owner of the stomach felt like passing out. Sometimes her stomach would whine and rumble in its agony. These mumbling sounds in Adah's stomach used to embarrass her no end. It was all right in Nigeria when she was a servant and an orphan, but it was uncomfortable when she was a woman in her own right and a mother of two!

She sensed that the hunger-pangs were about to start during her lunch break, so she decided to go for a walk instead. It was wet outside, and the staff-room was cosy and warm. The girls had already sat down and were talking of their conquests and, as usual, about marriage. She was beginning to agree with them that some marriages could lead to happiness, because the girls talked of nothing else but the happy ones. Well, hers was not happy, though she still believed that a happy marriage was an ideal life for a girl. One of the girls, Cynthia, was engaged to be married, and was sure hers was going to work. Adah had agreed with her so many times that she was no longer in the mood to listen to her happy chatter that day. Cynthia would notice her rumbling stomach and offer her some food, and ask her if she was all right and all that, so she would go for a walk.

She usually walked along Finchley Road, looking at all the restaurant windows she passed. She used to tell herself that, when Francis qualified and she had become a librarian, Francis would bring her to such places to eat. She sensed that, in her case, it was an empty dream. Even if Francis did qualify, he would never have the courage to bring her to a restaurant to eat, not in London anyway, because he firmly believed that such places were not for blacks. Adah knew that his blackness, his feeling of blackness, was firmly established in his mind. She knew that there was discrimination all over the place, but Francis's mind was a fertile ground in which such attitudes could grow and thrive. Personally, if she had had the money, she would have walked straight into such places and was sure she would have been served. But what was the point of her dreaming about it, she had no money! So she feasted her eyes on the well-displayed food. One particular item attracted her that afternoon. It was a fishcake in a fish shop. The cake was yellowish brown all round and very appetizing. Her mouth started to water like that of a starving dog, so she turned away. The uneasiness she had felt early in the morning seemed to descend on her again with so much force that she felt she was going to choke. For no reason whatsoever, she started to hurry back to the library. When she reached it, she would have a drink and a rest before going back to work. Thank goodness it was one of her early days. She would be finished by five.

She met Cynthia at the front door of the library, struggling hurriedly into her light summer raincoat.

'Thank God, you are here. I was just going to look for you.'

'My children. What's happened to them? Are they all right?'

'How did you know?' Cynthia asked, frightened. 'Who told you?' she went on asking as she trotted behind Adah into the library.

Yes, how had she known? How could a mother tell another

63

woman who had never given birth to a baby that sometimes she lived in her children? How could she explain that if her son underwent an operation her own body would ache, how could Adah tell Cynthia that when she was looking at the fishcake, she had seen Vicky's wet face, twisting in pain, reflected in the window? There was too much to explain; too much about herself as a human being, that she did not know. She just felt these things.

Adah did not cry. Victor was in danger, but not dead, and as long as he was alive, God would help him.

'You haven't heard the message?' the other assistant commented.

Then Adah got the message she had already sensed. Trudy had phoned, they said; Vicky was very ill and she couldn't send him to a hospital because she was waiting for Adah to come home.

Mrs Konrad, God bless her, drove her to the station. Adah ran from Kentish Town station to Trudy's house. There was an ambulance waiting outside the door. A small crowd had already gathered, talking, arguing and conjecturing. They all knew Adah, they'd seen her bring her children to Trudy's many a time. Titi looked at her pathetically as she ran past into Trudy's sitting-room.

Trudy was holding Vicky, wiping his face with a rag as filthy as an old mophead. She dipped the rag in a bowl of equally filthy water and rubbed it all over Vicky's face. She said she was cooling his temperature. A big bald doctor stood there, his bag in his hand. The Indian doctor with whom Francis and Adah had registered was too busy to come and the big bald fellow in black three-piece suit was his locum. He stood there, this doctor, looking at Trudy's ministrations objectively, as if they were no concern of his.

When Adah came in, Vicky lifted a hand and called his mother. He still knows me, Adah thought, as she scooped him from Trudy. She held him tightly, as if by doing so she could breathe health into the sick boy.

'What is the matter with him?' she asked, first the doctor and then Trudy. Getting no answer, she turned to Miss Stirling, who just stood there wringing her hands. If they knew what the matter was, they were not going to say.

'The ambulance is waiting. You'll find out in good time. Meanwhile we have to get him to hospital as quickly as possible,' the doctor ordered.

Though there was an urgent tinge in the doctor's voice, by Adah's calculations Vicky was not very ill. He was hot, running to a hundred and one in body temperature, yet Adah did not feel that there was any need to panic. She was thinking that Vicky probably had a bout of malaria, which to her was just like a common cold. Malaria would make a child's temperature run high, and it would go down as soon as the child was given Nivaquine. In fact, if Vicky had had the attack at home, that was what she would have done. As far as she knew, judging from the experience she had with Titi, children suffered only from malaria. Why all the panic then? she wondered. Any mother could cure a child of malaria without phoning the ambulance men or calling the doctor, who simply stood there, ready as if for nothing but to sign a death certificate.

'Vicky, say "bye-bye" to Trudy,' she said as they made their way to the door. Vicky waved bye-bye weakly, and also sang it, in his peculiar way.

They all – Trudy, Miss Stirling and the doctor – opened their mouths as if to tell her that the baby was too weak to talk. But they kept quiet when Vicky talked. Adah felt triumphant. Her son was simply running a high temperature, that was all. He was not dying, so they might as well get used to the idea. She felt like Jesus, who amazed His dumbfounded disciples when He said, 'Lazarus is not dead, he sleepeth.'

The big doctor saw through her agony, her fear, and touched her shoulder gently as she was about to step into the street. 'Your little son is very ill. I don't know what it is, but I am sure they will do their best for him at the Royal Free Hospital.'

Adah thanked him, but she was determined not to be made unhappy, not to be talked into expecting the worst. 'I think I know what the matter is,' she boasted. 'I think it is malaria. Children do have it at home, you know, just as you have common colds.'

'This may not be malaria, you know,' the doctor cautioned as he and the ambulancemen helped her into the ambulance.

In the ambulance, her thoughts were confused. Her brain worked tick-tock, as they say in Yoruba. Whenever anyone was thinking fast, he would say that his brain worked like a talking clock. She wondered what could be wrong with a child who had said 'good-bye' to her that morning. What could be so wrong as to merit an ambulance and a doctor? In Lagos, one had to be either a millionaire or a relative of the doctor's to warrant his visit. He wouldn't come just for a child running a high temperature. Now an ambulance was speeding her to Royal Free, just for that. Why was the name of the hospital Royal Free? Was it a hospital for poor people, for second-class people? Why did they put the word 'free' in it? Fear started to shroud her then. Were they sending Vicky to a second-class hospital, a free one, just because they were blacks? Oh, God, what had she let herself in for? They might even use her child's organ to save the life of another child, who would probably be white and rich and who would be admitted into a hospital that had no 'free' in it. A paying hospital. Adah did not then believe in anything good coming from something you did not pay for. She viewed anything free with suspicion and reluctance. In Nigeria, you paid for your treatment. The fatter your purse, the more intensive your treatment. She had never seen or heard of a place where a child was given such close attention by adults, free. There must be a catch somewhere. By the time they arrived at the hospital she was convinced Vicky's innards were going to be taken away from him.

The thought had got such a hold of her that she at first refused to let him go. Two nurses held her and took her into a small room with soft chairs lining the wall. They made her a cup of tea, with plenty of sugar in it. She drank it greedily with thanks, enjoying the taste of sugar which she hated normally. She had hardly ever had sugar because African mothers thought that sugar and meat caused worms. She had later come to like eating meat, but she never really acquired the taste for sugar. But on that day at the Royal Free, she was too hungry to care. She did enjoy the tea, and was told to wait while Vicky was being examined. She waited and waited, until she nearly fell asleep. Then she started to worry about Titi. She hoped Francis remembered to go for her. It was funny, really, she hadn't thought of looking for Francis. She did not want him to be worried; it wasn't anything serious. As far as Francis was concerned, she was still at work, and Vicky was at Trudy's.

Something kept telling her that she should let her husband know. But how could she when she didn't know where he would be at that time of the day? He had stopped attending regular lectures and just read on his own. That meant he could be in any library in London, or he could be with any one of his girl-friends. Adah was the last person to disturb him if he were busy on any of these preoccupations. She would tell him everything when she got home.

The nurse and two young doctors came to her. They told her that Vicky was very ill, but they'd taken all sorts of samples from him, and, until they got the results, they could not treat him. They would keep him under observation in the hospital.

To Adah, hospital usually meant two things. Where you go for your baby to be born or where you go when you're about to die. The first time she had been admitted to a hospital was when she was going to have Titi. The only other person in her family she knew had been in a hospital was Pa. He had gone for a check-up and never came back. These thoughts chased each other through her mind, as she tried to think of the right decision to make. She sensed, somehow, that she had little choice in the matter. Vicky had already been allocated a room, an isolated room, in case his illness was contagious.

She was allowed to go in and see him. He had been tucked in nicely, in a blue cot with blue fluffy blankets. He was not asleep, but stared at his mother as somebody having a bad migraine might. It seemed as if he found it difficult to move his eyes. Could they be right after all? Was Vicky very ill? She clutched the railings of the cot.

She was being watched through the glass partition. A nurse came to her and told her that it was time for her to go; Vicky needed rest and sleep. Adah nodded, and said good-bye to him, but Vicky did not answer; his tired eyes seemed to be gazing at something which only he could see.

Adah was not allowed to linger, she had to go.

Why, she thought to herself, didn't the authorities permit the mothers of young babies to stay with their sick offspring in hospital? In Nigeria, where the weather was warm enough, she could have stayed outside the hospital, under a big tree in the compound. Now she didn't know what she was going to do. Wait in the corridor? They would shoo her off. But, until then, that was what she was going to do. Fancy admitting a year-old baby into a hospital and not giving him any treatment because they were still diagnosing the symptoms. Suppose the child was seized by convulsions, as her children used to be when they ran a high temperature? The nurses would only pump injections into him, but she had seen babies suffer from these malaria seizures all through her life and knew all the first-aid cures. The hospital might not, so she would stay.

Adah dozed off on a wooden bench. When she opened her eyes, she was surprised to see the beautiful nurse with the soft voice who had told her previously that it was time to go.

She looked at Adah for a long time, and then smiled.

'Is Victor your only child?'

Adah shook her head, Vicky was not, there was another, but she was only a girl.

'Only a girl? What do you mean by "only a girl"? She is a person, too, you know, just like your son.'

Adah knew all that. But how was she to tell this beautiful creature that in her society she could only be sure of the love of her husband and the loyalty of her parents-in-law by having and keeping alive as many children as possible, and that though a girl may be counted as one child, to her people a boy was like four children put together? And if the family could give the boy a good university education, his mother would be given the status of a man in the tribe. How was she to explain all that? That her happiness depended so much on her son staying alive.

'Do you know, I'm making another one!' she volunteered, to show the nurse how good a wife she was.

The nurse, who either did not understand, or whose idea of a good and valuable wife was different from Adah's,

68

nodded but said nothing.

If Adah did not go, they would send for her husband, she said. She had to go.

Adah said she would only go if they used force, and so long as they were not going to do that, she was going to stay. But she went down to the corridor below, and watched some West Indian housewives coming to do their cleaning jobs.

Later that night, Francis came. Titi was spending the night at Trudy's, so he had come to look for her. For a while, it seemed as if Vicky's illness might bring the parents together again. Francis did not tell her not to worry, because he did not know how to do such things, how to be a man. Instead he cried, like a woman, with Adah.

Three days later, it was discovered that Vicky had virus meningitis. So Adah read all about the horrible thing, with its horrible unpronounceable name, in the library; she studied the causes, and knew all the effects.

'But where did he get it from? We never heard of such things in my family, and I never heard Ma mention it to me in your family either. Where did he get it from then? I want to know, because I'd like to prevent it in future, if he has any future, that is.'

'They cure everything here,' Francis replied, gazing into space.

'His chances of surviving are very slim, from the statistics I checked in a medical encyclopaedia. I want to know where my son got this virus. The medical books say he must have taken it through his mouth. I am very careful with Vicky and have not made as many mistakes as I did with Titi. I want to know where he got it from, and look, Francis, I don't care what you think any more, I am going to find out. From Trudy.'

'What's come over you?' he demanded, not believing his ears. 'What's happening to you?'

'You want to know what's happening to me? I'll tell you. You will have to know sooner or later. If anything happens to my son, I am going to kill you and that prostitute. You sleep with her, do you not? You buy her pants with the money I work for, and you both spend the money I pay her, when I go to work. I don't care what you do, but I must have my children whole and perfect. The only thing I get from this slavish marriage is the children. And, Francis, I am warning you, they must be perfect children.'

Francis looked at her, as if with new eyes. Somebody had warned him that the greatest mistake an African could make was to bring an educated girl to London and let her mix with middle-class English women. They soon knew their rights. What was happening to them? Francis wondered. In their society, men were allowed to sleep around if they wanted. That gave the nursing mother a break to nurse her baby before the next pregnancy. But here in London, with birth control and all that, one could sleep with one's wife all the time. But he was not brought up like that. He was brought up to like variety. Women at home never protested, and Adah had said that she did not mind, but, feeling the intensity of her anger, he sensed that she did mind. No man liked his freedom curtailed, particularly by a woman, his woman. He would not argue, he would not beat her into submission because of the baby, but he was not going to be tied to Adah, either. Why, in bed she was as cold as a dead body!

Adah was still talking. She was going to Trudy. She was going to get the truth from her, if it killed her.

'God help you,' Francis said. 'This is not home, you know. You can be jailed for accusing her falsely. You will be in trouble if you go and fight a woman in her own home, you know. After all, she is keeping Titi for us.'

'Yes, I know she is keeping Titi, so that you can pretend to go and see her at eleven o'clock every night. Last night you left at eleven, and you did not come back until I was ready for work. Seeing Titi!'

An uncomfortable pause followed, during which Adah seemed to be weighing up her freedom. After all, she earned the money in the family.

She continued, in a strange threatening way: 'If she does not give me a good answer, I shall bring Titi home with me and I am not leaving this house to work for you until the kids are admitted into the nursery or you agree to look after them. I don't care what your friends say. I am going to Trudy. She has something to tell me.'

'You're just like your mother after all. That quarrelsome troublemaker! People say women grow up to be like their mothers. But unfortunately for you, you're not as tall and menacing as she was. You're small, and I'm sure Trudy will teach you a lesson or two.'

'We'll see,' Adah replied as she dashed out of the house in a rage.

'They said at the hospital that Vicky had virus meningitis. And he is still on the danger list. I want to . . .' Adah began.

But Trudy cut her short.

'Yes, I phoned the hospital and they told me that. So I told them that you had brought him to London only a few months ago. He could have caught it from the water you drank at home, you know, before you brought him here . . .'

Adah stared at her; she could not believe her ears. Was she dreaming? What was it Trudy was saying about the child she had had in the best hospital in Nigeria, in the best ward, under the most efficient Swiss gynaecologist that the Americans could get for her as a member of their staff, which was one of the innumerable fringe benefits attached to working for the Americans? She wanted to explain all this to Trudy, but at that moment she saw Titi, coming in from the back yard, as filthy as the last time. Adah never knew what came over her. All she knew was that she lost control of the situation. Her inner eye kept seeing kaleidoscopically Vicky and Titi in the rubbish dump in Trudy's back yard. She could not eradicate that picture, rotating in her mind, and she did the only thing that came to her instinctively. In front of her was an enemy, insulting her country, her family, her person and, worst of all, her child.

Somebody had left a carpet-sweeper by the door. (Adah later wondered why this was so, because there was no carpet in either of Trudy's two rooms.) Without thinking, she picked it up, heavy as it was, and banged it blindly in the direction of Trudy's head! Trudy saw it coming and dodged. Somebody, another neighbour of Trudy's who was standing in the doorway, held Adah from the back.

'Don't, don't, don't do that,' this neighbour's voice came from behind her, cool, rational, reassuring.

Adah spat, foaming in the mouth, just like the people of her tribe would have done. Among her people, she could have killed Trudy, and other mothers would have stood solidly behind her. Now, she was not even given the joy of knocking senseless this fat, loose-fleshed woman with dyed hair and pussy-cat eyes. She belonged to the nation of people who had introduced 'law and order'.

Her tummy began to ache, just like the onset of indigestion. Adah was not used to bottling up her anger. Why, hadn't Pa told her that it was bad for the system? So to let off steam, she threatened:

'I am going to kill you. Do you hear that? I am going to kill you, if anything happens to my child. I shall sneak in here and kill you in your sleep. If not, I'll pay people to do it for me, but, believe me, I am going to kill you, and with a smile on my face. I saw Vicky with my own eyes in the rubbish dump. I smelt of you through my husband. I pay you with the money I earn, let my husband sleep with you, and then you want to kill my son!'

Then Adah broke down and started to cry, her voice coming out like that of somebody being tortured, strangled and harsh. The other white women stood there looking at her, shocked. They had probably never seen an angry Ibo woman.

If they were surprised, Adah was more than that; she was horrified at her own behaviour. She could not control herself any more. She had had so many things to bottle up inside her. In England, she couldn't go to her neighbour and babble out troubles as she would have done in Lagos, she had learned not to talk about her unhappiness to those with whom she worked, for this was a society where nobody was interested in the problems of others. If you could not bear your problems any more, you could always do away with yourself. That was allowed, too. Attempted suicide was not regarded as a sin. It was a way of attracting attention to one's unfortunate situation. And whose attention do you attract? The attention of paid listeners. Listeners who make you feel that you are an object to be studied, diagnosed, charted and tabulated. Listeners who refer to you as 'a case'. You don't have the old woman next door who, on hearing an argument going on between a wife and husband, would come in to slap the husband, telling him off and all that, knowing that her words would be respected because she was old and experienced. Instead you have the likes of Miss Stirling, whose office was along Malden Road in front of Trudy's house. Mercifully somebody had called her, and she arrived, breathing hard and blinking furiously.

She listened patiently to Adah's story, and appeared to agree with her, but said nothing about it. Instead she was quiet for a while, as Adah looked round at these strange people. Nobody blamed her, or Trudy. No speech. Adah felt like a fool. She was learning. People here do not tell everything; they don't say things like: 'I even allow my husband to sleep with her as part of the payment.' She noticed one thing, though; Trudy looked as if somebody was forcing her to eat shit. Her mouth went ugly, and her eye make-up was running in streaks all over her face. Even her black hair showed some strands of brown.

Then Miss Stirling spoke. 'We've got nursery places for the children. Your little girl could start on Monday and, when the baby is out of hospital, there will be a place for him too.'

Adah had exploded another myth. Second-class citizens could keep their children with them, but just look at the price they had to pay! Vicky was still in danger, her marriage hung in the balance, and now all this row.

She did not know whether to feel ashamed or grateful. She felt both, in a way, especially as it now seemed that her threats had been empty. There was no need for them.

She would not apologize to Trudy; that woman was a rotten liar anyway. They removed her name from the council list of approved child-minders and, still scared of Adah's threats, maybe, she left Malden Road, and moved to somewhere in Camden Town, so that if Vicky had died, Adah could not have carried out her threats.

She left the group, and walked home, crying quietly to herself. It was a cry of relief.

6 'Sorry, No Coloureds'

One morning, when Adah was rapidly tying her colourful *lappa* around her thickening waist in her haste to catch the train to work, her husband, who had gone out of the room, came in walking as if in a trance. He looked dejected, disappointed, and Adah thought she saw his hands shake. She looked up, the string of her *lappa* still between her lips, and her eyes started to beg for an explanation. Francis was not unaware of this, but for the time being he seemed to have decided not to tell her anything. Instead, he flopped down on the only available sitting place in their room – their unmade bed.

'Sad news,' he spat out eventually, as if he had a poison that tasted bad in his mouth. He reminded Adah of a snake spitting out venom. Francis had a small mouth, with tiny lips, too tiny for a typical African, so when he pouted those lips like that, he looked so unreal that he reminded the onlooker of other animals, not anything human.

Adah, knowing him, did not hurry him. He might decide not to tell her at all, and then her whole day would be ruined with wondering what on earth it could be. So she took her time.

'What sad news?' she asked, her heart thumping between her ribs. She was making a frantic attempt to make her voice sound unhurried, normal. Anything for a quiet life.

Francis held up an envelope, an impersonal type of envelope, one of those horrible khaki-coloured ones that usually herald the gas bill or the pink statement from the London Electricity Board. In any case, that type of envelope never brought good news to anyone.

'It is very, very bad news. And, believe me, I am beginning to lose faith in human nature,' he went on, savouring Adah's suspense. She was not surprised to hear the latter statement from Francis. He was always disappointed in human nature when other humans refused to bend to his wishes. He now sat there, smacking and resmacking his little wet lips, like a toy mouse-trap.

Adah could no longer bear the suspense. She was impatient, and was beginning to hate it all. She hated being treated like a native woman who was not supposed to know the important happenings in her family until they had been well discussed and analysed by the menfolk. Well, Francis could not do that, not in their one-room apartment, he couldn't. So Adah wanted to know immediately. She threw caution to the wind, walked menacingly towards her husband, snatched the envelope to the amazement of the latter, opened it and ran her eyes through the contents.

The message was short, to the point. No meandering.

A certain solicitor, representing their landlord, would like them to quit and give up all claims to the tenancy of their one room in Ashdown Street. And within a month!

This left a harrowing emptiness inside her.

Adah left the letter on the table, and went on dressing. There was no need to ask each other what they were going to do, because there was nothing they could do. Adah had known the notice would come. She had not actually had an open confrontation with any of the tenants, neither had she had any disagreement with the landlady, because she did everything to avoid such clashes, but there were many factors working against her. In fact, to most of her Nigerian neighbours, she was having her cake and eating it. She was in a white man's job, despite the fact that everybody had warned her against it, and it looked as if she meant to keep it. She would not send her children away to be fostered like everybody else; instead they were living with them, just as if she and Francis were first-class citizens, in their own country. To cap it all, they were Ibos, the hated people who always believed blindly in their ideologies. Well, if they were going to be different from everybody else, they would have to go away from them. When the fact of Vicky's admission to the hospital became known, everybody kept looking at Adah with an 'I told you so' sort of sympathy. Even the childless landlady was able to take the news that Adah was expecting her third with equanimity because, at the time, she was sure that Vicky was going to die. Instead, three weeks later, Vicky had arrived home from the hospital, weak, but alive and with a nursery place waiting for him. This was more than they could bear. Adah and her husband must go.

It was a surprise to Francis, because he thought that by confiding in them and adapting to their standards they would accept him. But he was forgetting the Yoruba saying that goes, 'a hungry dog does not play with one with a full stomach'. Francis forgot that, to most of their neighbours, he had what they did not have. He was doing his studies full time, and did not have to worry about money because his wife was earning enough to keep them going. He could see his children every day and even had the audacity to give his wife another. One never knew, Adah and Francis might even have another boy. They should go as far as possible from Ashdown Street. They knew how difficult it would be for them, but that was the desired effect.

Thinking about her first year in Britain, Adah could not help wondering whether the real discrimination, if one could call it that, that she experienced was not more the work of her fellow-countrymen than of the whites. Maybe if the blacks could learn to live harmoniously with one another, maybe if a West Indian landlord could learn not to look down on the African, and the African learn to boast less of his country's natural wealth, there would be fewer inferiority feelings among the blacks.

In any case, Francis and Adah had to look for another place to live. If it had been possible for them to find a new place, they would have moved within weeks of her arrival in London. But it had not been. During the days and weeks that followed, she had asked people at work if they knew of anywhere. She would read and re-read all that shop windows had to advertise. Nearly all the notices had 'Sorry, no coloureds' on them. Her house-hunting was made more difficult because she was black; black, with two very young children and pregnant with another one. She was beginning to learn that her colour was something she was supposed to be ashamed of. She was never aware of this at home in Nigeria, even when in the midst of whites. Those whites must have had a few lessons about colour before coming out to the tropics, because they never let drop from their mouths the fact that, in their countries, black was inferior. But now Adah was beginning to find out, so did not waste her time looking for accommodation in a clean, desirable neighbourhood. She, who only a few months previously would have accepted nothing but the best, had by now been conditioned to expect inferior things. She was now learning to suspect anything beautiful and pure. Those things were for the whites, not the blacks.

This had a curious psychological effect on her. Whenever she went into big clothes stores, she would automatically go to the counters carrying soiled and discarded items, afraid of what the shop assistants might say. Even if she had enough money for the best, she would start looking at the substandard ones and then work her way up. This was where she differed from Francis and the others. They believed that one had to start with the inferior and stay there, because being black meant being inferior. Well, Adah did not yet believe that wholly, but what she did know was that being regarded as inferior had a psychological effect on her. The result was that she started to act in the way expected of her because she was still new in England, but after a while, she was not going to accept it from anyone. She was going to regard herself as the equal of any white. But meanwhile she must look for a place to live.

Every door seemed barred against them; nobody would consider accommodating them, even when they were willing to pay double the normal rent. She searched all she could, during her lunch hours and on her way home from work. Francis would then take a turn. They had one or two hopeful experiences, but they were rejected as soon as it was known that they had children.

The landlord and the landlady were walking on air. They had got the proud couple down at last. They started to complain about everything. When the children cried, the landlord would stamp upstairs, warning them that they were disturbing the other tenants. The landlady, still childless, claimed that Adah was showing off her children. Why must Adah allow them to toddle about when she came out to fetch water? She must lock them up in their room. The landlady complained to her husband that Adah was bringing them downstairs to distress her.

Adah did not know what to do about this. If it looked like showing off, she was very sorry about it, because she knew what her Ma went through when she didn't have another child after Boy. Due to this childhood experience, Adah learnt to keep her pride in her children to herself. She was always wary of telling another childless woman what Vicky or Titi said, though she could babble endlessly to other young mothers like herself. But what was she to do? She told the babies not to follow her about. But, pray, how could a mother tell her young children not to follow her about, when those children had been all day in the nursery, in somebody else's care? The only way the children could keep an eye on their mother was by following her about.

This was made more difficult because, though she cooked in their small room, the only tap water for the tenants was on the ground floor. This meant Adah had to go up and down a great deal. And when she was downstairs the children would call to her, wanting to hear her voice for reassurance. Well, you know how the voices of children of that age are, especially to the ears of people who have never had children and who are dreaming that, when they do, they will bring them up in such a way as to make them behave like 'decent' children from the very earliest age.

One of the peculiarities of most Nigerian languages is the fact that one could make a song of everything. Native housewives used this method a lot. If an older wife of a polygamous marriage wanted to get even with a younger rival who was the favourite of the husband, she would make up all sorts of songs about the younger woman. Many women would go as far as to teach their children these songs, which were meant as a kind of psychological pressure on the young woman.

Of course, at Ashdown Street, neighbours would start singing as soon as they saw Adah coming. Most of the songs were about the fact that she and her husband would soon have to make their home in the street. What use would her education be then? the songs would ask. To whom would she show her children off then? It was all so Nigerian. It was all so typical.

Matters came to a new head when the landlord got so fed up with them that he decided not to accept their rent. Only someone who had been in a similar situation would know what an emotional torture this could be. Adah and Francis had the solicitor's letters pouring in every week, counting down the number of their days for them, just like a blast-off day for astronauts. They knew they were not wanted, because they were Ibos, because they had their children with them, because Adah worked in a library and because they found it difficult to conform to the standard which they were expected to live by.

Meanwhile the songs and the laughs took a much more direct form. 'I can't wait to see them pack their brats and leave our house,' the landlady would say loud and clear along the hallway, to nobody, just like a mad woman roaming about in an open asylum. At the end of her proclamation, she would then burst into one of her improvised songs, sometimes dancing to them in a maniacal sort of way. All this jarred on Adah's consciousness, almost driving her crazy. She had to bear it without responding in kind because, having lived most of her formative years in a mission fee-paying school, she had long forgotten the art of hurling abusive songs at others. Sometimes, though, she would scream 'The Bells of Aberdovey' or 'The Ash Grove' at the top of her voice, but her listeners did not understand what she was singing about. And even if they had, the songs were as inappropriate as wearing a three-piece suit on a sunny afternoon in Lagos. This went on so much that Adah started to doubt her senses. She would laugh loudly at nothing, just to show her neighbours how happy she was. The funny thing about the whole situation was that she was not unaware of the fact that her showy behaviour was really uncalled for. But it seemed that, like Francis, she had lost control of the situation. Just like a person living with a madman would. You come to behave and act like a mad person if you are surrounded by mad people. Was that what people call adaptation? she wondered.

Two weeks later, on the noticeboard in front of the post office at Queen's Crescent, she read on a blue card of a vacant room. There was no 'Sorry, no coloureds' on it. Adah could not believe her eyes. And the vacant room was not very far from where they lived: just around the corner, in Hawley Street. To make sure the room would be kept for them, she decided to phone the landlady as soon as she got to the library. She would make sure she phoned when the other assistants were out of earshot, otherwise they would think her mad or something. She had it all planned in her head. She had worked and talked for almost six months in London, so she was beginning to distinguish the accents. She knew that any white would recognize the voice of an African woman on the phone. So to eradicate that, she pressed her wide, tunnel-like nostrils together as if to keep out a nasty smell. She practised and practised her voice in the loo, and was satisfied with the result. The landlady would definitely not mistake her for a woman from Birmingham or London, yet she could be Irish, Scots or an English-speaking Italian. At least, all these people were white.

It was stupid of her though, because the landlady would find out eventually. She was simply counting on human compassion. When the landlady found out that they were blacks, she'd beg her, plead with her to give them a place to stay, at least till after her baby was born. Adah was sure her plea would move anybody, forgetting that her plight had failed to move her countrymen.

The voice that answered the phone was that of a middle-aged woman. She sounded busy and breathless. Not a very cultured voice, rather like the voices of the shrieking women who sold cabbages at Queen's Crescent market.

Yes, the two rooms were still available. The rent was the exact amount Francis and Adah were paying at Ashdown Street. Yes, she would keep the rooms for them. No, she did not mind children. She was a grandmother herself, but her grandchildren were somewhere in America. Was Adah an American, the voice wanted to know? She sounded like one, went on the voice. She'd be very glad to have them, to keep her house alive.

It was all so friendly, so humane. But what would happen

when the landlady was faced with two black faces? Adah told herself that it would be better to postpone this discovery to the last minute. One could never tell, she consoled herself, the woman might not even mind their being black. Hadn't she thought she was American? Adah realized that perhaps she made a little mistake there. She ought to have jumped at the woman's suggestion and claimed to be American. After all, there were black and white Americans!

Meanwhile she walked, as it were, on air. The woman had invited her and Francis to come and that was all there was to it. Why expect refusal, when the woman had sounded so jubilant? On her way home on the platform at Finchley tube station, it seemed to her ears and mind that the train that curled gracefully into view was singing with her. Sharing her happiness and optimism. It was going to be all right, the silent passengers seemed to be saying with their eyes, not their mouths. In fact everywhere and everything seemed saturated with happiness.

It was nearing the end of summer. The wind that blew carried an autumnal nip. The leaves were still on the trees, but were becoming dry, perched like birds ready to fly off. Their colour was yellow approaching brown. One or two eager leaves had fallen already, but those were isolated ones, too few to matter. As far as Adah was concerned, it was still summer. The trees still had leaves on them. And that was all she cared about.

She banged at their front door impatiently. Francis came out, in his loose, unbuttoned pale green cardigan, his belly bulging like that of his pregnant wife. The tail-ends of his shirt were hanging untidily out of his grey trousers. He peered at Adah over the top of his rimless glasses, blinking angrily, wondering what it was that had taken hold of her to make her behave so audaciously in a house where they were still like beggars.

'Don't look at me like that,' she cried with joy. 'We've got a room – no, two rooms. She advertised for one room, but when I phoned, she said she had two vacant. And, guess what, we will have to pay only the same four pounds we pay here. Two rooms for us in London!'

All this was too much for Francis. He had either been

reading and concentrating hard, or he was sleeping before Adah's bang on the front door woke him. Either way, he was like somebody in a daze and it was taking him quite a while to come out of it. He succeeded in jolting himself into wakefulness.

'Who, er . . . what, er . . .? Just wait a minute. Who is this person offering us a room, er, er . . . two rooms. Is she all right? This woman. I mean . . . she's all right, isn't she?'

'Of course she is all right. We're going to see the rooms this evening. I told her we would come at nine. Janet will look after the children for us. We must take the rooms,' Adah explained, her voice ringing musically.

But Francis maintained that there was a catch in it somewhere. He went on probing Adah. 'You said you spoke to her. So she heard your voice, then? It's amazing, I must say.'

Adah hoped very much that the woman would take them. The joy on Francis's face was like that of a little boy. He always reminded her of little Vicky when he was pleased. She did not delude herself into expecting Francis to love her. He had never been taught how to love, but he had an arresting way of looking pleased at Adah's achievements. Adah hoped she would never stop achieving success. Maybe that would keep their marriage together until they got back to Nigeria.

Children used to be one of the great achievements Francis appreciated, but in London, the cost, the inconvenience, even the shame of having them, had all eroded his pride in them. As long as Adah could bring home little triumphs like this one, he would go on looking pleased.

Adah did not tell him that she had held her nose when talking to the woman, neither did she tell him that she chose nine o'clock because it would be dark and the woman might not realize in time that they were black. If only they could paint their faces; just until the first rent had been paid. She dismissed this idea, mainly because she knew that Francis would not play. There was nothing she could do but hope for the best. Even if it all failed in the end, she was thankful for the temporary happiness they were experiencing. Francis started calling her 'darling', talking to her just like ordinary husbands did to their wives. He even volunteered to get the kids from the nursery, so that Adah could do the cooking. It was like a stolen hour. She was even beginning to think that Francis might be in love with her after all. All she need do was to bring up surprises like this once in a while. She did not allow herself to think that they might fail to get the rooms. The disappointment would be too heavy to bear.

Janet, now very friendly with Adah, did not need much persuasion to come and baby-sit for them. She was as excited as Adah, and they spent the time before their departure speculating on how nice Adah's flat was going to look. For, said Janet, two rooms made a flat. Didn't Adah know?

The night air was nippy, but Hawley Street was only ten minutes' walk from Ashdown Street. At first, they walked quickly, burning with hope. But when they came nearer to Hawley Street, Francis started to blow his nose, lagging behind as if he were going to face castration.

He looked round him, the excitement of the evening still with him, and exclaimed, 'Good Lord, the place looks like a burial ground.'

Adah had to laugh. The laughter of relief. Yes, the house was in a tumble-down area with most of the surrounding houses in ruins, and others in different stages of demolition. The area had a desolate air like that of an unkempt cemetery. Some of the houses had their roofs ripped off, leaving the walls as naked as Eve with no fig leaf for cover. The bare walls could be tombstones or the ruins of houses bombed by Hitler.

Adah did not mind the ruins and demolition, because the more insalubrious the place was, the more likely the landlady would be to take blacks.

They knocked at the door. A woman's small head popped out of a window, like that of a tortoise sunning itself. The head was like a mop being shaken at them. The voice was high and sounded strained, as it had been when it talked to Adah in the morning. She could not tell the age of the woman from the small head, full of loose-hanging curls. But there was something she could tell: the owner of that head could either not see properly or was colour-blind. Or maybe

she actually did not mind their colour. Adah started to
shake, not from the nippy air but from that sort of cold that
comes from the heart.

'The rooms – the advertisement on the noticeboard,' Francis
yelled at the quivering head.

'Yes, shan't be a minute. Be down to show them to you.
Just wait a minute.'

Then the head disappeared. It was looking as if they were
going to be given the rooms. *God, please let it be so*, Adah
prayed. The two of them were too astounded for words. Adah
put both hands in her coat pockets, to cover her bulging
middle. She remembered she had not told the woman that, in
less than four months, there was going to be another little Obi
added to the group. That would be a problem for the future.
For the moment, she must cover the baby up.

They could hear the light steps racing down the stairs.
Even Francis was beginning to be confident. The woman
did not mind blacks living in her house. The steps tapped
down the hallway and the light sprung on. Now the day of
reckoning had arrived, thought Adah. The lights would
certainly show them up for what they were. Niggers.

The door was being opened . . .

At first Adah thought the woman was about to have an
epileptic seizure. As she opened the door, the woman clutched
at her throat with one hand, her little mouth opening and
closing as if gasping for air, and her bright kitten-like eyes
dilated to their fullest extent. She made several attempts to
talk, but no sound came. Her mouth had obviously gone
dry.

But she succeeded eventually. Oh, yes, she found her voice,
from wherever it had gone previously. That voice was telling
them now that she was very sorry, the rooms had just gone.
Yes, both rooms. It was very stupid of her, she condescended,
because she ought to have told them from the upstairs window. She would put their name down, though, because she
was sure another room was going to be vacant down the road.
She pointed to some of the waste land farther down. If
there were any houses in the direction of her pointed finger,
only she could see them. All that Adah and Francis could
see was tumbled-down ruins. She hoped they would under-

stand. The room had just gone. She was breathlessly nervous and even frightened as she explained.

Francis and Adah said nothing as the flood of words poured out. Adah had never faced rejection in this manner. Not like this, directly. Rejection by this shrunken piece of humanity, with a shaky body and moppy hair, loose, dirty and unkempt, who tried to tell them that they were unsuitable for a half derelict and probably condemned house with creaky stairs. Just because they were blacks?

They stood there, as if rooted to the spot. The frightened woman hoped they would go. She begged them once more to understand that the rooms were gone. Her little eyes darted in Francis's direction, and Adah was sure the woman was going to scream, for the look on his face was ugly. All the letters that formed the word 'hatred' seemed to be working indelibly into it, like carvings on a stone. He was staring at this woman, and he seemed to be looking beyond her. She started to close the door, firmly. She was expecting opposition, but none came. Adah could not even utter the plea she had rehearsed. The shock was one she would never forget.

'Let's go,' Francis said.

They walked away in silence. Adah could not bear it. She had either to start screaming or talking; anything that came into her head. She started telling Francis the story of Jesus. She went on and on, how they were turned out of all the decent houses and how Mary had the baby in the manger.

Francis looked as if he was in another world, not listening to her. There was nothing Adah could do but to keep talking and try to keep up with Francis, thought he was now walking fast, as if chased by demons. Then, all of a sudden, he stopped. Adah was startled. Was he going to kill her now, she wondered?

But he did not touch her. All he said was, 'You'll be telling the world soon that you're carrying another Jesus. But, if so, you will soon be forced to look for your own Joseph.'

'But Jesus was an Arab, was he not? So, to the English, Jesus is coloured. All the pictures show him with the type of pale colour you have. So can't you see that these people worship a coloured man and yet refuse to take a coloured family into their home?'

If Francis was listening, he gave no sign of it. He probably realized that Adah did need to talk, because he did not hush her. He seemed to be enjoying her voice, but his mind did not register what it said.

Exhausted, Adah stopped talking. They were near their home in Ashdown Street. It dawned on them that nothing but a miracle would save them now.

And what saved them was just like a miracle.

7 The Ghetto

There was another group of Nigerians who had come to England. This group of men came in the late forties, when Nigeria was still a colony. Even under colonization, they were men in the middle-class strata of Nigerian society. They were well educated, with good secondary schooling or its equivalent, qualified enough to hold down clerical jobs in the Civil Service. These were men who were conversant with the goings-on in world politics, who knew that colonialism, like the slave trade, would soon become too expensive for the colonial masters; that the outcome would be independence – in the same way the slaves were freed, when it became too expensive to keep them. The final nail in the coffin was the independence of India. It would soon be their turn. Nigeria would soon become independent.

These groups of men calculated that with independence would come prosperity, the opportunity for self-rule, poshy vacant jobs and more money, plenty of it. One had to be eligible for these jobs, though, thought these men. The only place to secure this eligibility, this passport to prosperity, was England. They must come to England, get a quick degree in Law and go back to rule their own country. What could be more suitable?

The reaction that followed this sudden realization spread like wildfire. Responsible men, in high Civil Service posts, threw up their jobs, asked for their gratuities, demanded their pensions, abandoned their children, gave twenty pounds or so to their illiterate wives, and packed their bags for the trip to the United Kingdom in search of eligibility. The eligibility that would make them free, free to rule their country, free to go into poshy jobs with long shiny American cars with back wings. The eligibility that would sanction their declaring their old illiterate wives redundant and would not frown on their taking one of the newly emerging graduate females in Nigeria as a wife. Oh, yes, there was a great deal the United Kingdom was going to do for these men.

In search of this dream or reality, or whatever you decide to call it, they sold all, abandoned all they had held dear. They were like those men in the Bible whom Jesus had told to sell all they had and follow him. Those men in the Bible had little to lose. Only their nets. But these Nigerians had plenty – wives, status, jobs and many, many children. The mothers of these children, though dubious about the whole plan, though they might have wondered what was to become of them and their offspring, dared not say anything, otherwise they would have been branded as wicked women who stood in the way of their ambitious husbands. Of course, the husbands promised to be better husbands to their wives, good and rich fathers to their children, men of whom they would all be proud when and if they came back from England. The children, poor things, were usually overjoyed at having a father in the United Kingdom. But whether they saw their father again, or whether he was a better father for his going to England, no one knew.

As is well known in such cases, many people were usually called, but few were chosen. Most of the first generation of Nigerian politicians, who sprung up from everywhere after the independence, just like mushrooms, were from among these men. Some of them actually made it; they came back to Nigeria, equipped with law degrees, and a great talent for oratorial glibness. They had mastered enough political terms to turn the basic proposition of having enough food for everybody into beautiful jargon, which left their listeners lost in the muddle of long, jaw-breaking words. Some of these listeners sometimes wondered whether they were not better off with the white master, who would at least take the trouble to learn the pidgin English which they could understand. Not to worry, though; being independent and learning to be a world statesman demanded certain things. One must be well-versed in rhetoric, whether it made sense or not!

However, most of those men who sought the kingdom of the eligibles did not make it. Like the seeds of that sower in the Bible, they fell on the wayside to be trodden upon by passers-by. They came, failed to make a foothold, in England, sought consolation in the pubs, got themselves involved with the type of woman who frequented the pubs – because it was just after the war, when many unattached women were around, and that, of course, meant good-bye to their Law studies and a happy welcome to a house full of half-caste children! Nearly all the failures married white women. Maybe it was the only way of boosting their egos, or was it a way of getting even with their colonial masters? Any woman would do, as long as she was white. The set of African males who started to discriminate between the educated and the uneducated white woman came later. But for those men who did not make it, educated or not educated, it did not matter; Irish or English or Greek, it did not matter. She was white. If they remembered or had pangs of guilt about their families at home, they stifled them with the consolation that, after all, they were married to white women. That, at least, would not have been possible at home. If they remembered their original dream, the dream of reading Law and becoming an élite in their newly independent country, they buried it deep in their bitter hearts. It was such a disappointment, too bitter to put into words. When these men fell so disastrously, their dreams were crushed with them. The dream of becoming an aristocracy became a reality of being a black, a nobody, a second-class citizen.

There was one old Nigerian, Mr Noble was his name – at least, Mr Noble was what they called him at that time, but Adah came to know later on that this was not the name his mother and father had given him. He was given that name when he came to England, when he became a second-rate person, when he became second-class. In the early sixties, when Adah came to know this man, there were all sorts of stories going round about him. The stories were so many, so confusing and so contradictory that he became a living legend. The version that was told to Adah was that he was a retired civil servant, that he was the only son of a certain chief in Benin City, that he had six wives and about twenty children and that he left them all, and came to England to read Law. The long and short of it was that he failed to make it.

His failure was due to a gross miscalculation. The pension and gratuity money he brought with him was not even enough to see him through GCE or Matriculation or whatever they called those examinations in those days. He kept failing and failing, and his money vanished, just as if he had gambled with it. But Mr Noble was undaunted. He would work and study. He searched for work in all the offices his disappointed mind could think of, but with no success. He settled, instead, on becoming a lift man at a tube station. His work was to shout 'Mind the doors!' all day and to collect tickets and sometimes pennies from fare-dodgers. If he was disappointed with the work and the situation he found himself in, he drowned it in drink, frequenting pubs and night clubs. His mates at work were not bad. They liked him, because they turned him into a jester, a clown. They would invariably ask him to perform some African tricks, just for laughs, and Mr Noble would comply. Nobody knew what actually went wrong, but Mr Noble started to behave like a child. Who said that society makes us? Was it Durkheim? Well, if he had said so, or something to that effect, he was right in Mr Noble's case. He stopped being a man respected in his own right and became a clown for men young enough to be his sons. On one occasion, he was asked to remove his trousers; his mates wanted to see whether Africans had tails or not because that was the story they were told during the war. Adah remembered her father telling some of his friends something like that, but she had been too young to understand. When she heard of Mr Noble's case, she knew that such stories really were told. In any case, Mr Noble removed his trousers for a pint of beer. It was then that he became so popular, popular and generous enough to be given the name 'Noble'. He was such a noble man that he would do anything for his mates, even taking his trousers off!

So Mr Noble liked the name. It stuck to him like a leech. He found that by claiming to be Mr Noble, things became a little easier for him. At least he had an English name. But his clownish performances nearly sent him to his Maker one quiet afternoon. Adah did not really know what had happened. The story was too illogical even for fiction. But people believed that was what had happened. Mr Noble had his shoulders to show as proof, so there must be some truth in it.

The story was that one afternoon, when it was not very busy in the lift, one of Mr Noble's mates told him to operate the lift manually, without the electricity provided. Mr Noble had always told them that Africans were very strong. On this afternoon he was told to prove it, for a pint of beer. Mr Noble stooped, like a big fool, to shoulder the lift. Only God knew how his muddled brain told him he could do this but, nevertheless, he attempted it to prove how strong he was, for a pint. Something in the lift groaned, twisted and crashed on to him, trapping his shoulder. His mates got scared. Some made as if to run, but two or three could not deaden their ears to the soul-rending bleating of Mr Noble. The sound was awful. It was like the sound men might make if they were being dismembered alive, just before they lost consciousness. His mates tried to help him. They heaved and puffed at the lift door, but Mr Noble's shoulder was trapped among the twisted metal. Help came eventually, and he was rushed to hospital. He was not operated on, but that right shoulder was useless for life. It later affected the whole arm, so much so that on seeing him one would at first get the impression that he was a one-armed man. The shoulder was permanently dislocated.

The railway authorities were very generous. They paid him a lump sum in compensation for his injury. It was treated as an accident at work. All his mates came to the court to testify on his behalf. So Pa Noble was pensioned off for the second time.

This time he decided to face reality. Hope of his ever becoming a learned lawyer was fast disappearing, so he invested his money in buying an old terrace house in Willes Road, just by Kentish Town station. He could only afford the cheapest, for he did not wish to be saddled with endless mortgage. He could not anyway get a mortgage, so had to buy cash down. Mortgages and things like that were for the fully employed, the young and, at that time, mainly for whites.

There was a big trap in buying the house, but at that time he was carried away with a big wave of optimism and he fell into it. The house had three floors, and the two top floors were occupied by two sisters who had been born in the house. When Pa Noble heard of this, he told himself that the two women were bound to move out as soon as they knew that their new landlord was a black man. He was wrong. He did not know what it meant to be a rent-controlled tenant. He thought that owning a house in England was like owning a house in Nigeria, where you had more freedom with your property. He had never heard of a situation in which the landlord was poorer than the tenants. He did not know that the law could be so strong on the side of the tenant. He bought the house, dreaming of all the improvements he was going to make with the big rent he was going to collect when the white sisters moved out.

But the two women not only refused to move, they refused to increase their rent, which was less than a pound a week for the two floors. Mr Noble went several times to the Town Hall at Euston to moan about his fate, but there was nothing the clerks could do. It was the law. You could not evict a controlled tenant, you could not increase their rent, not even when you wanted to use the money for improvements. Mr Noble felt like going crazy.

That was not the end of his trouble. He stopped going to the pubs, but not before he'd got himself one of the women who frequented them. This woman – Sue was her name – started to do her bit, blessing Mr Noble with more and more children. It came to a point where there was no place for these children to sleep. Mr Noble went to the court again, but he lost. The old ladies were controlled tenants. He must not evict them, even though the forty-year-old son of one of the women lived with his mother and was a junior manager in an office. He refused to pay more rent to Mr Noble.

Mr Noble came to the end of his tether. Having lived most of his life in Nigeria in a village where most people knew how to use psychological pressures on one another, Mr Noble decided to use this type of pressure. He told the old ladies that his mother was the greatest witch in the whole of Black Africa. He told them that he had reported them to this great mother of his, and that she was going to kill them. He kept making a song and dance of this information, even when he saw the old ladies in the street. If they were frightened, they pretended they were not. But Mr Noble knew that they were beginning to be afraid of him. He was on safe ground, because these poor old things, who were caught in the same situation as he was, could not prove his psychological cruelty in the court. They pretended to ignore him. Meanwhile, Mr Noble told everybody who would listen that he had reported the old ladies to his dead mother. Many Africans took him seriously, because such things were possible at home. But the Europeans who heard him ruled it out as the ravings of a crazy man. His wife, Sue, was amused by it all.

Then the great winter of 1962 – 3 came. The weather was so cold that many old people could not even come out to leave their empty bottles for the milkman. The walls of Mr Noble's house started to feel the strain of the weather. He could not repair it because the old ladies did not pay enough rent. One of the old ladies died. Mr Noble shouted that his dead mother was acting on his behalf at last. The cold weather did not give up. It continued. It snowed without cease for weeks. In one of the cold weeks that followed, the other sister died. The son fled in terror.

Mr Noble boasted, 'I told them so. My old mother killed them from her grave.' But what Mr Noble did not tell his friends was that the roof of the house leaked, that the stairs were cold and that they creaked, that the walls were damp and that the windows were cracked. So the story clung. It became the thing to talk about his power in hushed tones. Everybody knew that Mr Noble could kill.

He enjoyed the popularity which this story gave him for a while, but stopped enjoying it when he saw that nobody would live in his house. The house was too old, too shabby for any white family. So he was calculating on his fellow Nigerians snatching up the empty rooms. He was not unaware of the housing shortage. But people were always hesitant about living there. The few who did, did so just as a stop-gap until they found somewhere else. Nobody wanted to stay for long. So Pa Noble's rooms were almost invariably empty.

Francis and Adah heard that Pa Noble had a vacant room. They knew about the dead sisters; they heard about his

93

great power over others; they also knew that his wife Sue was a filthy woman who invariably stole bits and pieces from their tenants. But what were they going to do? Adah's baby was due in a few months, winter was fast approaching, and their present landlady would not change her mind. Adah did not at first like to take Janet's hints and talk to Francis about their going to see the Nobles. She went on hoping it would never come to that.

But it did come to that; when they had only two days of the extended time given to them by the landlord's solicitor left, she decided to talk to Francis about it. She made sure she chose the right moment. These moments were usually when Francis was pressed with desire for her. She would encourage him to work himself up and then bring up important discussions like where they were going to live. On this particular occasion, Francis was like an enraged bull.

'Why must you talk about it just now at three o'clock in the morning? Why, you wicked witch? Is it too much for a man to want his wife?' he thundered, shaking Adah brutally by the shoulders.

She whimpered in pain, but she was not going to give in. Not until they had discussed the Nobles and decided where her baby was going to be born. It was all right for Mary to have hers in the stable in Bethlehem, but that was ages ago and in the desert, where it was always hot. Not in England where it could be as cold as a mortuary in winter, or so Adah had been told. Francis must be made to talk about it, and this was the only way. Three o'clock in the morning was the only appropriate time. It was a time when it was too late for Francis to run to any of his girl-friends for help; it was the time when only Adah could meet all his wants; it was the only time when she and she alone, of all the women in the world, could satisfy him. Adah knew how vulnerable Francis could be at that time, so she sat by the edge of the bed, sparsely dressed, covering her head with her hands and looking down at her bulging midriff.

Her voice too was part of the act, low, and hushed, but she pressed her point. 'Are we going to see the Nobles or not?'

'Yes, yes, we will,' answered Francis quickly rushing to

her. She dodged, and this annoyed her husband and he demanded: 'What the bloody hell do you want? I've said that we will go and talk to them, what else do you want?'

Adah was now standing by the sink and felt like laughing at Francis, standing there all flushed. How like animals we all look when we are consumed by our basic desires, thought Adah, standing there by the sink, like a wicked temptress luring her male to destruction. All that Francis needed to be taken for a gorilla was simply to bend his knees.

'Yes, I heard you, but I want us to go there tomorrow, so that we can move by the week-end if possible,' she said, maintaining her ground, her large, tired eyes lowered. If she looked up, the magic would stop working.

Then Francis went on, pleading like a fool, 'Oh, yes, we'll go tomorrow. Is that all you wanted? Have I ever refused anything you said? Are you not like my mother to me in this country? Have I ever refused your command?'

Adah had to laugh here. Her command, indeed! How funny men can be! Her laughter was mocking, but Francis took it for a laugh of acquiescence. She might as well give in to him, now, otherwise it would result in blows. She accepted what came to her after that, for the rest of the night, hoping and praying that her baby would not be born three months prematurely. She heard the church bell chiming seven o'clock, when Francis rolled on his side, like an exhausted drunk. It was all over, but they would see the Nobles.

It was a damp windy day in September. Autumn was on its way already. It blew the cold rain on to their faces but their hearts were panicky and their steps uncertain. Still they went on. They were going to the Nobles'. Francis had not forgotten his promise of the night before.

Willes Road was narrow, curving into Prince of Wales Road. Approaching the street from the Queen's Crescent side, it had a gloomy and unwelcoming look, but the part that joined Prince of Wales Road widened into a cheerful set of well-kept Edwardian terrace houses with beautifully-tended front gardens. Those houses, the clean, beautiful ones, seemed to belong to a different neighbourhood; in fact, a different world.

As was to be expected, Mr Noble's humble abode was situated in the middle of the gloomy part. There was a mighty building curving right in the middle of the street, shutting away the cheerful side from the gloomy one, as if it were determined to drive the poor from the rich; the houses from the ghetto, the whites from the blacks. The jutting end of this building was just like a social divide; solid, visible and unmovable. This building, built with red bricks, was a school or something and it pointed right in front of Mr Noble's house, so that one side of it faced the good side of the street, and the other the forbidding side. His house needed no description. 'Just go to Willes Road, ask for the black man's house and it will be shown to you,' Janet had said, and she was right. Francis and Adah had little difficulty in finding the house. It was unmistakable.

It looked the oldest house in the street, sandwiched between two houses owned by some Greeks. These houses were old, too, but had been coated with fresh paint and the front gardens still had flowers in them. The windows had white net curtains and their doors had brass knockers. Mr Noble's house looked like a midget between two giants. His was neglected. The front garden contained piles of uncleared rubbish and the fence needed mending. The whole house needed a coat of paint.

Francis banged the curved, blackened knocker. The knock was faint and uncertain and was swallowed up by the music blaring from the television. It was the time when the Beatles were still handsome young boys doing their 'He loves you, yeah, yeah' stuff. The 'yeah, yeah' was echoing from the house. Francis would have to knock harder. Adah felt like telling him so, but decided to be quiet, otherwise they would go into the Nobles' house still arguing who was right and who was stupid.

The intensity of the knocks progressed from the first mild knock to the final thunderous one. The whole house shook and two curtained windows, on either side of the door, made funny moves as if they were hiding the curious. Francis looked desperately right and left, like a man who felt like running. Adah looked at him, her silent, sad face asking what he was going to do. Francis thought better of it. Maybe remembering the price he had had to pay for coming this far he decided to wait.

Then they heard a pair of feet shuffling on a lino-covered floor. The owner of the feet was not in too much of a hurry, he was taking his time, all right. The door opened a little, and someone peered at them through a small gap. The person stood there for what seemed centuries, deliberating, maybe, about whether Adah and Francis should be allowed in or not.

Then, all of a sudden, there was a funny laugh. The type of laugh one usually associates with ghosts in places like Tutenkhamun's tomb. It was like the sound made by an old frog. Mr Noble even looked like a black ghost, for his head was hairless, and he seemed to have dyed the skin on his head black. It was a while before Francis and his wife realized that the croaky noise was Pa Noble's way of welcoming them.

The noise subsided slowly, giving way to a smile on a face; the face of an old man. A face that had been battered by gallons of African rain; burned almost to scorching point by years and years of direct Nigerian sun; and later on ravaged by many biting wintry winds in England; a face that was criss-crossed like a jute mat by bottled-up sorrows, disappointments, and maybe occasional joys. It was all there, on Pa Noble's face, just like an indelible legend written by Mother Nature on one of her sons. He had a hollow in the middle of his neck. Two prominent bones formed a triangle which encased this hollow, and whenever Pa Noble talked, something that looked like a chunk of meat inside his gullet would dance frighteningly in this encased hollow and the onlooker would feel like begging him to stop talking. He reminded them of a dying old man eager to tell it all to the living world before he passed to the other side and his voice was silenced for ever. To press home his point, which he did very often, Pa Noble would gulp.

He opened the door wider, welcoming them. It was then that he displayed his hands. They were so claw-like, those hands; they were wizened, blacker than the normal black, in fact they looked like burnt clumps, with tiny, equally black fingers attached to them. As for the dislocated arm, it reminded anybody of those unfortunate Thalidomide kids. He came nearer to them, to have a better look at his two visitors. It was then that he removed his large square glasses and peered again and again, like a blind bat. His eyes were deeply set inside deep hollows. Adah could not see the whites of those eyes properly, but nevertheless she got the impression that she was being looked over by a pair of very wise and very old wicked eyes. They were so sharp, so precise, even though they were set so far back. Adah recoiled from Mr Noble's effusive welcome. The words and sentences he uttered were warm but those eyes, that face, that laugh! Adah prayed to God to make Mr Noble put on his glasses again. At least that would cover up the two hollows. Was that why he wore glasses in the first place, to cover the skeleton-like cavities? He certainly seemed to see better without them.

God heard Adah's silent prayers and Mr Noble replaced his glasses. He had on layers and layers of clothes, vests, shirts and old jumpers and on top of it all an old grandpa God-forsaken coat with sagging pockets. The trousers looked as if they had originally belonged to somebody bigger than him; on him they hung loose like the clothes of a television marionette. The feet were covered with folds of wollen socks, which sagged on his ankles, the elastic grips having been long exhausted. The whole lot, the feet and the tired socks, were stuffed into two large, ill-matched slippers. One of the slippers was made of brown leather, the other was made of blue canvas. The man looked exactly as people described him – like a witch-doctor.

'Come in, come in, *iyawo.*' *Iyawo* is a Yoruba word for a young wife, not necessarily a bride. Adah must have looked quite young to Mr Noble. 'Come in, and welcome,' he said, showing his gleaming teeth. God was merciful. Giving such a perfect set of teeth to such an ugly old man. Those teeth added life to his face, making it show traces of humanity.

He drew Adah and Francis towards him. They entered the hallway and waited for Pa Noble to shut the door.

All of a sudden, another voice rose above the sound of the

television, louder than the Beatles. The voice was a woman's, loud, authoritative and direct.

'Papa! Papa! Papa! Who is it? Who is it, Papa? Papa ... Pa ...'

'Visitors!' Mr Noble croaked, his old voice almost cracking in the attempt. The lump in his throat danced furiously. 'Visitors,' he repeated, this time in a lower key, as he ushered the two trembling figures into the sitting-room.

The overheated room, the blaring television, the airless atmosphere all combined to greet them in one big whiff as they went inside. The room was small. A large double bed took up a considerable proportion of the room. Opposite the bed was a table on which were clustered all sorts of children's articles: feeding bottles, a plastic plate, clothes. In the centre of this jumble stood the majestic television, trumpeting away as if determined to make its presence felt amidst the sobering jumble. Children's litter was accumulated everywhere, on the floor and on the chairs; even the walls were not spared from little smears. Piles and piles of clothing in different stages of cleanliness lay in uncomfortable places. A child was sleeping on the bed, apparently too tired to be disturbed by the noise. Sitting very near the child, with her feet stretched straight in front of her, was a woman. Mrs Noble.

Mrs Noble was a large-boned Birmingham woman, still young and still pretty, with masses of auburn hair hanging loose about her shoulders. Her blue eyes were direct and candid and looked as if they were determined to find out straight away what Francis's and Adah's business was. Those eyes were always suspicious of people. That hair of hers, hanging long and thick, and curly in parts, made her look like a wild gipsy beauty. If she had had earrings on, Adah would have sworn that Mrs Noble was the very woman who approached her weeks before at Queen's Crescent, telling her that she would be lucky with men and that she would have many boy-friends. Her eyes were now peering at them, from her wide face, seemingly unsure of how to receive their visitors. Adah involuntarily had to say 'Hello.' She made a great show of mouthing it, because the television was still blaring. She gave a wobbly smile as well.

Mrs Noble's eyes leapt into action. They danced humourously, their centres twinkling like distant blue waves on a sunny day; she shouted, welcoming them as if she had been waiting for them all her life. She jumped up smartly, surprisingly nimble for her large bulk, from the bed of jumble and started to fuss over them, her eyes bright and laughing all the time. She was warm-hearted, kind, friendly, loud, and unreserved; the type of woman who would not hesitate to tell you the first thing that came into her head.

Her visitors relaxed though, mainly due to her.

Mrs Noble got busy. She lumped together two or three piles of clothes, some damp, others dry, to make room for Adah and Francis. She made a blind dive into one of the damp piles, fished out a towel, rubbed it energetically over two straight-backed chairs, and invited them to sit down.

Pa Noble took Adah's white coat which he hung on a nail behind the door. Francis refused to take off his coat because of his shabby jumper, so he sweated in the heat. It was then that Adah realized that she had made a mistake in allowing her coat to be taken. What would these people say when they realized that they were not just visitors but prospective tenants? They could see that she was pregnant, they would soon know that she had two other children as well. All that was not going to be easy to explain away. Maybe they had not noticed. So she made frantic attempts to do her breathing exercises. She held in her bulge, feeling the pain. She would relax after they had made their inquiries.

Mrs Noble was determined to play the role of the perfect hostess to the very full, quite oblivious of Adah's thoughts.

'Oh!' she exclaimed as Adah was settling on the chair provided. 'Oh, that chair is too hard for you.' Adah jumped. The woman's eyes had not missed a thing. Would Adah like to sit on the bed, it was much more comfortable, much softer, 'you know what I mean.' She gave Adah a good wink of her blue eyes, a wink that was meant to be conspiratorial. But Adah looked blank. But Mrs Noble roared with laughter. Whether she was laughing with or against her, Adah could not tell. But she learned later on that whenever Mrs Noble felt she had cracked a joke, she laughed like that, forcing her listeners to laugh with her whether they saw the joke or not. Her laughter went on and on so that even Francis, who seldom smiled, had to join in. She was so infectious, that woman.

Tea was served in chipped cups and mugs. Adah's arrived in a big mug, over-sugared and too milky.

'You must drink for the two of you,' Mrs Noble explained kindly.

Adah shrank back with fear, avoiding Francis's eyes. Adah thanked her aloud, but in her heart she consigned her to her Maker. If only she would stop her natter, the air would be cleared for them to proceed with their request.

But Mrs Noble did not stop, she talked about everything, but about nothing in particular. She seemed to feel that she would be failing as a hostess if there was any silence at all. She drew Adah into the orbit of her topic by asking her if her children had started taking English food. This surprised Adah, because she did not know that the Nobles knew they had other children. They probably also knew why they were paying them this visit. Their Nigerian neighbours had been doing a great deal of gossiping.

'No, they have not taken to English food much, but they are fond of chips,' replied Adah.

'All children like fish and chips. Ours will not take boiled or roast potatoes, but you fry them and away they go, just like that! I think children all over the world like fish and chips. It's an international food, not just English,' Pa Noble said absentmindedly, his eyes focused on the television.

His wife looked at him curiously and asked: 'Papa, did you eat fish and chips when you were little?'

Papa, who until then seemed to have forgotten their existence, leapt back to life. He took out a small tin of snuff and administered the stuff to his wide nostrils, then wheezed and sneezed, then jolted himself upright and put the snuff tin back into one of his sagging coat pockets, clapped his claw-like hands in an unnatural sort of way, hunched up his stiff shoulder and rubbed his hairless head. His wife sat back nicely, making herself comfortable among the piles of clothing, relaxed, ready to be amused.

Papa Noble told them that he was born in a tree. His mother fed him on breast milk until he was almost twelve. He had to be weaned because he was by then old enough to join the menfolk in the farm work. He never wore clothes until he was taken into the army. Yes, he said, all children in Nigeria were brought up like that. There was no food, people died of dysentery every day. He ate meat only twice in the year during the yam festival and the festival of his father's gods. In fact, he only started to live when he came to England. And, of course, he started to enjoy life only when he met his Sue.

'Why did you not tell your wife that your father had tails, Pa Noble?' Adah blurted out. She felt sick. Why must Pa Noble descend so low? Just to be married to this woman?

Mr Noble simply laughed, or rather croaked, '*Iyawo*, you are very, very young and inexperienced. I hope you'll learn very soon.'

'She's only a woman,' Francis said by way of an apology.

Mrs Noble had been so amused that she started to laugh to herself. Francis, who like Pa Noble always had a certain tenderness towards any white woman, smiled at her. It seemed as if their friendship clicked in that smile. Adah felt betrayed, but she knew something. They were going to get the room they were asking for. Pa Noble was too old for Sue.

8 Role Acceptance

One day, weeks later, when Adah, Francis and their two young children had settled in at the Nobles', Adah felt unwilling to go to work. She felt uncomfortable and unusually heavy. She could have stayed longer in bed, but she had to be in the library by nine-thirty. Sad, and feeling very sorry for herself, as she usually did on such days, she dragged herself up, envying her husband who was still having a good snore. She felt like waking him up, just for the sheer joy of it. She was stretching her hands towards him, on the verge of pulling him up, when the piece of humanity inside her gave her a gentle kick. It seemed to be saying to her, *What do you think you're doing, eh?* This gentle push was followed by arrow-like punches. One of the punches was so intense that she was jolted into reality.

According to her calculations, she should have the baby at the beginning of December. As a matter of fact, she could have the baby any time, because it was almost due. It was already December, the second day of the month. The baby would not come on the second, she told herself. The actual date was the ninth. So she was sure the child inside her was simply having a morning stretch. Do babies do morning exercises in their mothers' tummies? She must check it up some time.

But one thing was beginning to worry her, though. Her bulk. Her boss was always looking at her, when she thought Adah was not watching, wondering. Adah had lied to them, to the doctor, saying that her baby was due early in February, so that she could stay as long as possible at work. They would then have enough money to tide them over till she started work again. Francis had been convinced that it would be right for him to work during Christmas at the Post Office. So if only Adah could work as long as possible, they would be

103

able to pay their rent, pay for the children's nursery and put some money by until she got strong enough to go back to work.

Looking back at that time, she still wondered why she never thought it odd that she should be doing all the worrying about what they were going to live on, why she, and she alone, always felt that she was letting those she loved down if she stayed away from work, even for the sake of having a baby. The funniest thing was that she felt it was her duty to work, not her husband's. He was to have an easy life, the life of a mature student, studying at his own pace.

She got herself ready that morning, and hurried to Kentish Town station. When she got there, she realized that the railwaymen were having one of their go-slows. She did not know this, because she was so completely isolated from other people, that if not for her visits to her place of work, she would not have known anything that happened outside her home. Francis did not believe in friendship. The only friends he was beginning to cultivate were one or two Jehovah's Witness people, who came to their room once or twice. Their bags were so big that all they reminded Adah of were the Hausa meat-hawkers in Lagos. Adah did not mind them, they might even make a faithful husband out of Francis. But the Jehovah people could not tell her that there was going to be a rail strike. They never read the papers, it was a waste of money, Francis had maintained. They had neither radio nor television. They were completely cut off from any type of mass media. Though Francis infrequently went downstairs to Mrs Noble's to watch their television, Adah was banned from going there because the woman would be a bad influence on her. Adah did not particularly like Mrs Noble and was too busy with her own lot, so she did not make any protest. She simply accepted her role as defined for her by her husband.

There was a crowd of innocents there on the platform. Maybe they, too, like Adah were completely isolated from the goings on in society, or maybe they thought the railwaymen would have changed their minds in the night. The crowd waited, patiently, though muttering like angry bees.

The pushes and nudges inside her became more determined.

She wondered what the little devil wanted her to do. Scream right there on the platform? A kind huge gentleman with a bowler hat, dark suit, briefcase and tightly-rolled umbrella, vacated one of the wooden benches for her and motioned her to sit down. 'We may still have a long time to wait,' he said smiling. His great big face looked like that of a little boy. Adah thanked him. She was sure he was a headmaster of a boys' school. What gave her the idea she did not bother to find out.

She sat there. No train, but more nudges. The crowd started to drift away. One or two keenies went on peeping into the dark tunnel as if to conjure up the train. But no train came.

Adah knew by then that the railwaymen had been on strike that day for her sake. The pushes, though not constant, were too determined to be ignored. But what would Francis say? she wondered with fear. He would accuse her of laziness and would remind her that they needed her money. *Oh God, she prayed soundlessly, please give Francis a sign, any proof to make him believe me. As you can see, dear God, I am in pain. Not just shy of work, but in real pain.* Then she started to think again. Supposing she played it up. Started to scream as if the devil was burning her insides. That would be nice. She would get the sympathy she wanted. She decided that that was what she was going to do. Francis would be given the most terrible proof he had ever seen. Well, he was asking for it, and she was going to give it to him. She felt happy. God had heard her prayers. With that thought in her mind, she felt happy. The little person inside her seemed to be happy with her. It seemed to have forgotten how to kick. It seemed to be having its elevenses or something like that.

But how was she to start screaming when the baby was having its elevenses and she was feeling no pain at all? Should she start the pain, just to give her something to scream about? Another fear gripped her. She suddenly remembered that with the other babies she had had, screaming was as exhausting as having the child itself. She could hear the voice of her mother-in-law who kept telling her, when Adah was in labour with Titi, that women who screamed were cowards, that the more they screamed, the less energy they had left in them. So when it came to having their babies, they were sapped of strength, because they had drained all their energy away screaming like mad. Adah knew this to be true somehow. When she was pregnant with Titi, she had just left school and though they had taught her some health science, nobody warned her that first births take such a long, long time. That time she had screamed, not with pain, but with fear, because it was taking so long. And when the baby was actually born, she was completely unconscious. But with Vicky she knew better. She read and read, as if she were going to study medicine. So she knew what it was that was happening in every stage. All that knowledge seemed to have evaporated, somehow, because there was no mother-in-law to tell her what to do. Because, from what she had heard, in London the midwives gave mothers drugs and gas. The gas affair worried her somewhat. It surely would not be the same gas you use on yourself when you want to do yourself in? If it was, how would they know when she'd had enough? That would kill her, no doubt. Then she would not see the little person inside her, then she would not see Titi and Vicky grow up and go to school. Oh, no, it is all so unfair. When do they give one the gas? she wondered. She thought again. It's probably when you scream too much. England is a silent country; people are taught to bottle up their feelings and screw them up tight, like the illicit gin her parents drank at home. If you made a mistake and uncorked the bottle, the gin would bubble out. She had seen English men and women behave like humans once or twice, but why was it that they only behaved like humans when they were straggling out of the pubs on Saturday nights? Well, if they would give her gas to shut her up, then she would not scream. She would face Francis and have it out with him. She knew Francis, she'd rather have a fight with him than with a god or goddess she did not know. Because how was she to know where the gas thing would send her?

She went home. She told Francis why she could not go to work, how the railwaymen had gone on strike for more pay. She knew it was for more pay, because she had heard the angry murmurings of the impatient crowd of innocents on the platform. She told him how the man with the umbrella had vacated the wooden bench for her and how the slats of the bench had hurt her posterior. She told him how they had all waited hoping that by waiting they would somehow conjure up a train from its tunnel hole; she told him how it had all come to nothing, for there was no train, and everybody had gone home, including herself. She had had to come home.

Francis was still in his pyjamas. He heard her out, with his brow arched like a wicked spy in a James Bond film. Then he asked Adah how she knew that everybody had gone home. Did all the passengers tell her that, or was she making it all up? Was the story of the strike what she was cooking up when she looked down at him that morning when she thought he was asleep? He had seen her then. He thought at first that she was going to smash his skull into a pulp from the way she was looking at him with thick hatred. She should have thought of a better story. She should know though that she would make all of them suffer, including the person inside her and herself too.

Adah could not say anything. She did not know whether she had been wise in not choosing the other alternative. She ought to have decided on screaming and faced the gas and Jupiter or Lucifer or even the angels. The angels might even have welcomed her singing the 'Hallelujah Chorus' which she loved very much. Then the nagging constraint came again. What of Titi and Vicky? Well, the angels could wait. For now she was sure she was going to the angels; had not Jesus said that those who suffer here on earth would inherit the Kingdom of Heaven. She would like to go there some time, with her children. Francis could go where he liked. He could take care of himself.

The nudge came again, followed by the determined kicks and she felt like screaming, but she told herself not to, because the English midwife might give her gas and that might send her, not to the beautiful angels singing the 'Hallelujah Chorus' but to Lucifer with his horns of fire. Then, when Vicky got into a temper and spat out his Rice Krispies, and Titi was as silent as the tomb, refusing to talk, who was going to tell them that they were beautiful children? Who was going to tickle them till they laughed, and Vicky spat out more Rice Krispies all over her face, and Titi started talking, non-stop like a bad radio that had lost its switch? The angels could keep their heaven, and she, Adah, was staying right here by her children. Because, even though the baby was lying in a funny way, she was going to live to see not just her grandchildren, but her great-grandchildren as well. At least, if they were not all blown up to pieces by the bomb!

Then came the sermon. Francis was a great one for preaching sermons. It was always Jehovah God said this, Jehovah God said that. Adah was having a rest after the last onslaught from her baby, so, with eyes glazed like the eyes of the pig's head at the butcher's, she watched and listened to her husband preaching to her about the diligence of the virtuous woman, whose price was above rubies. This virtuous woman Francis was yapping about would wake with the first crow of the cock. Adah wondered where she was going to find a cock that would wake her up. But on went Francis, on the morning of that second of December. Jehovah God would bless such a woman. Her husband would be respected outside the gates. Adah wanted to ask which gates, but she was too numbed by the whole show. Fancy, she said to herself, Francis preaching to her the sermon of diligence at half past ten in the morning, when he was still in his pyjamas. She started to curse her mother-in-law for spoiling all her sons. There were so many girls in the family that the boys grew up thinking they were something special, superhuman creatures. Adah went on hearing about this virtuous woman whose price was above the rubies, but the sermon went in through one ear and came out of the other.

At least the joy of his listening to his own voice would let him leave her alone to ponder what it was she was going to do about this baby, whose legs seemed to be kicking not her front, as other babies did, but her ribs. This was making it difficult for her to breathe. She imagined the baby lying across, in the little cage made by her ribs, kicking away with careless abandon. Francis had said only two days ago that he had more ribs than she had, because Jehovah God took one of his own ribs and broke it into seven little pieces and made her own cage for them. That was why she was called 'wo-man' because she was made from the ribs of a man, like himself. It made sense when he was talking, 'woman' being an English word which may be regarded as a compound word, 'wo' and 'man'. What would be Francis's interpretation of the Western Ibo word for woman, *opoho* which had no relevance to the word for male *okei*? Francis would have to build another story for that, because the explanation for the rib structure would not apply at all. But he went on and on, about how Jehovah was going to bless the virtuous woman.

Adah had probably made a mistake, and allowed her disbelief to show on her face, for Francis accused her of not believing him. Did she think he was lying? Why was she looking at him like that? He got quite excited by this religious fervour. He would show Adah that it was all written in the *Word of God*. The *Word of God* was a book whose cover was of that cheap type of cloth which binders used in Lagos to bind children's ABC books. The pages of the book were made of paper the likes of which one would use for blotting paper. The difference between the leaves of that book and blotting paper was that blotting paper was bleached white, but the pages of this book were not white, nor yellow but were criss-crossed with brownish fibres like the veins of a hand. Inside this book were pictures of Adam eating the apple and Eve talking to the snake. They both had fig leaves covering their sex. They did not look too unhappy after eating the apple, though Francis said they were, otherwise they would have been without fig leaves. Covering themselves like that proved that they had known good and evil. Adah did not know what she was supposed to do now. Strip herself? Refuse to eat any more apples from the Crescent? Francis himself was clothed in pyjamas, which needed washing. The trousers were as big as the baggy trousers worn by Nigerian drummers, and his sex was inside these baggy trousers, dangling this way and that like the pendulum of Big Ben. She had never seen Big Ben, but she was sure that a big clock like that would have a pendulum. Francis's sex was dangling just like that.

It dangled much more furiously now, this way, that way, and back again, because he was excited. He was going to show Adah proof of what he had been saying about the virtuous woman. He was going to get the book called *The Truth Shall Make You Free*. He could not find it quickly enough. Adah knew he would start another sermon on Paradise, then he would ask her to read a passage, then he would ask her if she understood, and she would have to say, yes, she did understand it all right. He would then call her 'Sister', not wife, because Jehovah God ordained it so. Every female believer was to be called a sister and every male believer a brother. It did not matter whether the male was your husband or father. All believers were brothers and sisters. Sometimes Adah used to wonder whether God really said all that. One thing she did know was that the greatest book on human psychology is the Bible. If you were lazy and did not wish to work, or if you had failed to make your way in society, you could always say, 'My kingdom is not of this world.' If you were a jet-set woman who believed in sleeping around, VD or no VD, you could always say Mary Magdalene had no husband, but didn't she wash the feet of Our Lord? Wasn't she the first person to see our risen saviour? If, on the other hand, you believed in the inferiority of the blacks, you could always say, 'Slaves, obey your masters.' It is a mysterious book, one of the greatest of all books, if not the greatest. Hasn't it got all the answers?

But the one thing Adah could not stand was when a group of people took a portion of the Bible, interpreted it the way that suited them and then asked her to swallow it like that, whole. She became suspicious. She did not mind it if Francis believed it, except when it disturbed his studies or if either of the children needed a blood transfusion and he refused. The thought of this made her smile, because when she had needed blood, when she was having Titi, Francis forgot the Word and gave it. Francis was not a bad man, just a man who could no longer cope with the over-demanding society he found himself in.

He bent down double now, looking furiously for *The Truth Shall Make You Free*, throwing the children's clothes this way and that. Adah saw her scarf, made a dive for it and walked quickly towards the door. She heard Francis shouting, calling her back, because he had found the book. She must come back, he commanded, because he had not finished having his say. To Adah he sounded like Nero in *Quo Vadis* who accused his courtiers of dying without his permission.

Adah hurried, wobbling, to Dr Hudson's surgery at the Crescent. It was a horrid day; grey, with the sparse snow of the night before clinging to the ground. It could not melt because the ghostly sun that shone from among the heavy clouds was hazy; too hazy to have any effect on the stubborn snow. It made it very dangerous for Adah to walk. But, anyhow, she padded just like a duck, first to the right then to the left.

Maybe people passed by her wondering. They maybe wondered what it was that was the matter with her, walking like that, like a duck. Perhaps one or two people would have liked to ask her if she needed any help but got scared off by the determined look she gave them all. She walked on, and did not see the people.

She found a corner in the surgery and sat down. At least if she really felt like screaming here she could and nobody would think it odd. The thing that troubled her was that she had this pain which, disturbing though it was, was not bad enough to be the real labour – those hot ones that make a mad person of any woman. She did not understand it. The person inside her kept pushing her this way and that way, so that to sit down was trouble; to stand, trouble; to walk more trouble. So she sat on the metal chair in the surgery shifting her bottom about the seat like someone sitting on thorns. She fixed her eyes on the poster on the wall which said 'No Smoking' and explained how smoking causes lung cancer. There was a drawing of the ribs showing the fluffy lung inside it. Adah wondered whether that was the drawing of a man or a woman. How could one tell? Francis had said that men have more ribs than women. And not only did they have more ribs, but that one of a man's ribs makes all the ribs of a woman. Adah peered again at the drawing of the ribs and concluded that they must be those of a woman. The ribs were too fine, too regular to be a man's. Fancy a woman having to work, having to carry babies who kept pushing their mummies about and, on top of it all, having to have cancer as well. Was Eve the only person who ate the apple? Did not the man Adam eat some too? Why was it that women had to bear most of the punishments? It was not at all fair.

The patients started to trickle out one by one. She was not in a hurry to go. All she would hear at home would be Francis and his sermons. She was better off where she was. A woman who came after her with a baby as red as new carrots nudged her to go in. She replied by telling the woman to go before her. The woman with the baby told her that she came after her, not before. Adah told her to go in all the same. The woman was about to start her own sermon about Adah needing the doctor urgently. Adah ignored her, and started to puzzle out all over again whether the ribs opposite her belonged to a man or woman. The woman stared at her, just as if she were a crazy woman let loose from an asylum. She thought better of it and decided to take her red baby up to Dr Hudson. The waiting-room was now empty except for the domestic woman. She, too, had a red face, and a big stomach. She was not pregnant, because her hair was white and fluffy like cotton read; to be spun into thread. She smiled at Adah. The teeth were too close, too regular to be hers, but anyhow, the smile was nice. The charlady wanted to talk. Adah would have liked to talk to her, but how was she to know whether the lady had heard of a baby lying across the mother's tummy before! She decided against telling her anything. But the woman went on talking of this and that. Like Francis's sermon, it went into one ear and came out of the other.

The charwoman stopped talking because they could hear voices coming down the stairs, the voices of the doctor and that of the woman with the baby like a carrot. The woman with the baby must have alarmed the doctor no end, for she dashed to Adah calling her 'dear', leading her up just like a big egg that might break and mess the stairs all over. She led Adah into the surgery, and motioned her to climb on to the bed. Adah could not climb, and she was examined on a chair.

'Your time is too near to be comfortable. You should have phoned for the ambulance straight away. You need to rest now. I am sure you'll have your baby in less than twenty-four hours, if all goes well.'

Adah looked at her, scared now. Why must she go in an ambulance, when she had told her that she and Francis had decided that she would have the baby at home? Had not the hospital given them a list of what she was to buy for the confinement, and hadn't Francis demanded angrily whether she was preparing to get married, buying all that stuff? Hadn't Francis decided that the six pounds they would give her if she had the child at home would be useful? Adah had agreed with him. She would have the child at home and earn six pounds. There would not be any need to buy two or three nightdresses, no need to buy a housecoat, or bedroom slippers, and no need for a toilet bag. Yes, the six pounds would feed them for a week.

She told the doctor that she was not having the baby at University College Hospital but at home in their room at Willes Road. The doctor asked her why she had changed her mind, seeing all the trouble she had taken in booking her in at that particular hospital because the waiting list was long. Did Adah not know that the food was perfect there, and that she could do with a bit of a rest from her family? How was Adah going to cope anyway? She only had one room, didn't she? Then what had got into her head to make her refuse to go into hospital? Did Adah not know that many women would jump at the chance?

The doctor went on talking. She was a great one for talking, the doctor. She was angry now, washing her tiny hands, wishy, wishy wishy, squeezing one small hand against the other, wishy, wishy. Adah followed her movement with her eyes. What a day for sermons, she thought. But the doctor's sermon did not go in one ear and out of the other. Adah listened and allowed the words to sink down into her mind. How was she to tell Dr Hudson that she had to have the baby in their one room to earn them six pounds, because the six pounds would feed them all for a week, maybe for eight or nine days? The doctor would only ask her why it was that her husband did not go out to work and earn the six pounds. And to answer that, Adah would have to tell the doctor woman that her husband believed in Armageddon. So there was no need for him to exert himself too much in this world, otherwise he would lose his share of the kingdom. The tale would be too long, and the telling of it would make her cry. So she let the story be. She just told the doctor that she would rather go now, since she had to get Francis to phone the widwife. The doctor sighed. She told her to hurry home. She would do the phoning.

Somehow, Adah managed to get home. The journey had taken such a long time, with a rest here and a sit-down there. She rang the bell, because, in her hurry to leave Francis, she had forgotten her key. She scolded herself for this. She was always forgetting her door key in England. In Africa she seldom carried one: your door was always open. In the afternoon, people would all be out on their verandas, talking and eating sugarcane, coconut or bananas. In England people locked themselves inside; they made a paradise of their living-rooms, because they didn't stay out a lot, not like they do in Africa. Francis was always reminding her to take her key whenever she went out; one day Mrs Noble might be in one of her moods and refuse to open the front door for her. What would she do then? She would have to stay out and freeze. Just like that Lot's stupid wife who did not do what she was told but kept looking back all the time, and was turned into a big lump of salt. That lump must have been a big one. Did people make soup with that type of salt, salt made of a woman? Eerr, it would be nasty salt, that. She was happy that she was not born in Sodom and Gomorrah.

She rang the bell again, this time pressing it long and hard. She did not care now if it annoyed Mrs Noble or Mr Noble or even Francis. She did not care any more. What she did care about was Francis getting annoyed and appearing in his cheap linen pyjamas, with the baggy trousers and his thing in it swinging this way and that way because he had no underpants on. Adah prayed to God to inspire Francis to remember to put on his woollen dressing-gown. The dressing-gown fitted well; it was new, for he had bought it here in England. But the pyjamas, though they had a 'Made in Great Britain' label, were bought in Lagos. Adah wondered who told them in Britain that people in Lagos could do without superior things. She remembered looking at some of the biscuits Mrs Noble was giving Kimmy, her black dog. She had touched the biscuits and, had it not been for the fact that people were watching her, she would have tasted one. Were those not the very ~ame type of biscuits sold to people in Africa, and were those not the very ones her Pa and her uncles used to bring for her and her brother Boy from the army barracks when the war was over? Anyhow, they had not died; they had even thrived, for those hard, dry sugarless biscuits were good exercise for their teeth when they were kids. Did they still sell such biscuits in Lagos, when the devils had taken hold of the Japanese and they were pouring luxury foods and articles into Lagos at two a penny?

She prayed harder now, because up the road she saw two women riding madly on two grey bicycles checking the numbers of the houses. She saw their black shapeless coats and black hats. Their shoes were black and shapeless too. Just like men's shoes they were. Adah guessed that they were the midwives coming to help her deliver her baby. Mistakenly they passed her, but Adah did not call them, for that would give her a few minutes in which to ring the bell once more and to tell Francis to cover himself up with the woollen dressing-gown if he was still in his wrinkled pyjamas. Her prayers were answered, for Francis came down, hasty in his anger, but he had not only taken off the linen pyjamas, he was dressed for the day in his grey flannel trousers, cream coloured shirt and his pale green cardigan with a criss-cross pattern on it. Just as he was about to open his little Chinese mouth to ask her what it was she thought she was doing ringing the bell like that when she was supposed to carry her key like a talisman all the time, the two midwives realized their mistake, and wheeled their grey bicycles, cheering themselves like two children who had discovered a hidden treasure. They did not mount their bicycles, but pushed them along, the chains making sounds like 'tuk, tuk, tuk'. The two owners were grinning from ear to ear as they trotted along, their bicycles beside them like lame horses. One of the midwives was English; the superior air was unmistakable. Her hair was white, at least that part of it that had escaped from under the black hat. She was big-boned, in her forties and had a determined look. The other woman was her assistant, younger and foreign. She could be Japanese or Chinese, because she had a pair of those peculiar eyes that

115

seemed to be sunk into people's heads. The young woman had a face as round as a perfect O. Her mouth and nose were too small for her face.

The grin left the faces of the two women as soon as they realized that she was Mrs Obi.

'Can't you read English?' asked the older midwife with the white hair. It dawned on Adah that, to the big midwife, if you couldn't read or speak English, then you were illiterate. Adah did not want to be regarded as an illiterate, so she told her that she could. Then the big midwife with white hair and authoritative air asked her why then had she not called them sooner? Had Adah not read the instructions that she was to call her at the onset of pains? What did she think she was doing, being so bloody clever?

'Rook, rook, she's breeding,' gasped the young nurse with the face like an O.

Adah tried to puzzle out what this statement could mean. Yes, she was breeding, definitely. She was having her third baby, but everyone knew that. Why should the nurse make so much noise about it? If she were not breeding, she would not have called them in the first place.

The big midwife who had probably worked with her assistant for some time understood her perfectly. For she went on: 'That's what I mean. Can't you see that you are bleeding profusely? Come on, up to bed.'

Did 'breeding' mean bleeding for the Japanese nurse, when she said 'rook', did she mean 'look'? Adah was learning.

They went on examining her, digging into her. One finger, two fingers, three fingers; on and on they went, talking in low voices in their special code, or so it seemed to Adah. Her pains did not get more acute, but all of a sudden she could take no more. Francis, who caused it all, standing there staring, like a pig's head at the butcher's, standing there at the foot of the bed, just like a referee impatiently waiting for fair play. Adah remembered then that she had read or heard of husbands who became panicky and worried in case their wives died. But not Francis. He was sure Adah would live. To him Adah was immortal. She had to be there, bearing his children, working for him, taking his beatings, listening to his sermons.

The room started going round and round in all the colours of the rainbow. Francis had now turned into Lucifer. His wicked eyes were glazed as if he wore badly fixed contact-lenses, he was wearing a robe of fire, he had horns bigger and more complicated than those of a stag, and his swords were emitting flames. He was telling her that she was being punished for not waiting to read *The Truth Shall Make You Free*. Her running away to the doctor woman was causing her all this pain. Then the voices of the two women floated in . . . one finger, two fingers . . . then she heard the word 'dilated' or 'dilation' used over and over again. Then somebody covered her nose and mouth with some rubber stuff. So they were gassing her . . . Francis's voice kept on and on, counting down like the persistent bells of death. So this was death, this was what it felt like . . .

She could not have the baby . . . Too big for her, poor thing. Then in came Francis again. If she had not interfered with his pleasures with Trudy, if she had been a good wife, a virtuous woman whose price was above the rubies . . .

She heard the bells, the ambulance bells. But they jingled as if they were Peter's bunch of keys to heaven telling her that she could only hear the jingles of the keys of heaven, but she would never go there. She was going to her Lucifer husband with the horns of fire. Somebody, two men or even three, were lifting her on to something. She opened her eyes; they were descending the creaky, Noble stairs.

Then she saw Vicky, clutching at Mrs Noble's breast, his little face confused. Adah saw the fat cheeks, the pathetic baby eyes, and prayed to God to send her back whole to her children. She wanted to call out to Mrs Noble to tell her to wipe Vicky's running nose, to tell her to pull Titi's pants up, because they were coming down – the elastic was slack and she had forgotten to put in a new piece. She could not. Her mind was talking, but her mouth could not. The ambulance men in black suits had her all wrapped in flaming red blankets, and they were hurrying her. The voice of the big midwife was urging them on . . .

Adah sank back into the world of dreams.

The dreams were like before. Trouble. She could not run to her husband for help because he was still carrying that

117

sword of fire. She could not see Peter with the keys, but she could hear the bells ringing, ringing. Sometimes she heard the voice of the big nurse, saying, 'Hurry, hurry, we must hurry.' Then the voice of the little nurse said, 'Good Rord.' She tossed this way and that way, running round in circles. To run to Peter, trouble; to run to Francis trouble.

So she ran round and round, until a big, mighty voice cut through to her: 'You know what we are going to do, madam; we are going to get the baby out for you. It is just a little prick and you won't feel any pain.' The big voice was still talking and another moist hand was scratching her thigh with something needle-like. She felt it all, but did not see anything. Then peace descended like a shower of blessings.

There was peace everywhere. She had had the baby and it was now a boy of five. Francis was no longer a Lucifer, but a prosperous farmer. They had their own house, large with spacious rooms, airy verandas. She was sitting on the veranda sipping the extracted juice of some ripe mangoes. They were talking and laughing. She and Francis. Francis was reminding her of their terrible time in London. And she was laughing, laughing and laughing . . . because it had happened such a long time ago when they were very young. But now it was all over. Titi was in a convent school in England and Vicky was at Eton. There were other children as well, but they were too young to go to school abroad. They were staying with them, wanting this and wanting that. Francis was so happy and was coming over to her cane chair, kissing her very, very softly, telling her how virtuous she was and how her price was above rubies. And how all the other farmers for miles and miles around had sold all their farms to him and how he now was the lord and master of several farms, miles and miles around. What more could a man want than a virtuous wife like her who had helped him achieve all this?

Then the trouble came back with the word 'virtuous'. On and on rolled the word. Then all the colours of the rainbow appeared again, red, blue, yellow, pink; you name it, it was there, all the rainbow colours, and on each one was written 'Virtuous'. Virtuous and more virtuous, so many of them. So confusing. Virtuous here and there, so confusing was the riot of colours and virtuousness that she did the only thing that came into her head. She screamed, high and loud.

On and on the screaming went. She would never stop.

Then she stopped all of a sudden. Somebody was smacking her on her thigh. That somebody was calling her 'madam'. That somebody was urging her to wake up now, because they had finished. She tried her eyes; yes, she could open them. She surveyed her surroundings. The men and women were like angels of light, clothed in white. They were smiling down at her, lying there, not covered in flaming red blankets this time, but in clean white sheets, soft and immaculate. The only person with a splash of blood on him was the big man. There was no doubt about it. He was the person who had cut her open, to take out that funny baby that had lain across her, instead of lying straight like every other child. She thanked the big man with her eyes, for she was still weak from screaming, and from the cutting open. They sensed that she was asking them for her child.

They brought him. He was so big and so hairy that Adah was at first frightened. He was not only big and hairy like a baby gorilla, but hungry like a wolf. He did not cry like other babies, he was too busy with his mouth, sucking his big fingers, swallowing the wind. Good Lord, was that the child inside her all the time? Thank God they got him out in time. He was so hungry, he could have eaten up her insides.

'You've got a boy,' the nurse that was holding him said unnecessarily.

She smiled her thanks to them all and drifted into a peaceful sleep.

9 Learning the Rules

Adah awoke to find herself in a big open hospital ward. She was on a bed at the extreme end of the ward, next to the door. Surveying the whole scene with her tired eyes, she recalled her old school's dormitory. But instead of the beds containing young, black giggling girls, these beds contained women. Some were not very young, but most were young mothers like herself. They were talking, or most of them were; one or two were trying to read magazines. The conversations around her went in buzzing, buzzing. These women were all happy and free. They seemed to have known each other for years and years.

She was ashamed of herself, because somebody, she did not know who, had decided to make a fool of her. She was lying there, all tied up to the bed with rubber cords, just like the little Lilliputians tied Gulliver. There was a rubber tube running from her arm connected to a bottle of something like water. The something like water inside the bottle dripped, a drop at a time, and the drip would run through the tube and into her arm. Or so it seemed to her. This drip was on the right-hand side of her.

On her left was a big balloon-like bottle, white and clear. Inside this otherwise-clean bottle, like the ones used for making wine in, was some muddy water. The water contained some soot in it. The water looked like the running sooty water on a railway line on a wet day. They, these invisible people, had tied her to this sooty bottle. They allowed a rubber tube joined to it to run through her nose, to the back of her mouth. To talk was difficult; to move was impossible. She simply lay there, trying to puzzle out why she was being singled out for this treatment.

As if all that was not enough, a young nurse marched in with a stand, like the one attached to the bottle with the drip, and stationed it near her head. Another nurse soon followed, carrying a bottle half-filled with blood.

'Ah, so you are wide awake. Good!' the first nurse said by way of greeting.

The other one looked up from under Adah's bed where she was screwing the nuts for the other stand and greeted her with a watery smile. 'I don't think we'll need this, but just in case,' finished the second nurse. Both of them, nurse number one and nurse two, had turned the bottle of blood upside down, attached it to another tube, but left it like that. 'We may not need it, but just in case,' nurse number two had said.

The nurses walked out briskly, as briskly as they had come. Adah turned her eyes to the woman on her right, and the woman smiled and asked her how her tummy was feeling. Adah tried to answer back, to tell her that at that moment a kind of mincer had been stationed inside her tummy by some angry gods; to tell her that this mincer seemed to be bent on turning everything inside her into a neat pulp; to tell her that the bottle with water attached to her left arm was placed there by those nurses and doctors to help the mincer mince her insides very quickly; to tell her that while all this mincing and dripping was going on, her body was hot, her lips parched like a desert wanderer and her head swinging round and round like the tub for spinning cotton. But Adah could not say a word. The rubber tube that passed through her nose to her mouth had seen to that.

They were kind, those women in the ward. For the first few days, when Adah was deciding whether it was worth struggling to hold on to this life, those women kept showing her many things. They seemed to be telling her to look around her, that there were still many beautiful things to be seen, which she had not seen, that there were still several joys to be experienced which she had not yet experienced, that she was still young, that her whole life was still ahead of her.

She would never forget one woman, who looked the same age as Adah's Ma. This woman had been married seventeen good years, and she had had no children. Never miscarried. And then all of a sudden God decided to visit her, just as He visited Sarah, the wife of Abraham, and she became pregnant and she too had a son. This woman never stopped showing this child around, even when she was not strong enough to walk properly. Adah did not know that the woman had had to wait seventeen years for her son, and she got tired of admiring this baby with thick brown hair which stood out angrily like electric wires. She was the more annoyed because the tube in her mouth did not give her any freedom to talk to the woman, to tell her that everybody in the ward had had a baby or was expecting one, to ask her what it was that was so special about her little son anyway, showing him around like that as if he were a prize or something. But, thank God she never had the opportunity to say this. Four days later, when the tube was removed, the woman next to her, whose husband looked old enough to be her father, told her that the woman with the baby with the wiry hair had had to wait for seventeen years to have a son. Adah gaped. Seventeen good years! She wanted to ask all sorts of questions. What did her husband do, for instance? She imagined herself in the woman's position. Waiting and waiting for seventeen years for a child that was taking its time to make up its mind whether to come or not to come. She tried to imagine what her life with Francis would be if she had given him no child. She recalled Titi's birth. After a long and painful ordeal she had come home to Francis bearing a girl. Everybody looked at her with an 'is that all?' look. She had had the audacity to keep everybody waiting for nine months and four sleepless nights, only to tell them she had nothing but a girl. It was nine good months wasted. She paid for it, though, by having Vicky soon afterwards.

Suppose she had had to wait seventeen years for all that? She would have either died of psychological pressures or another wife would have been bought for Francis. He would have declared himself a Moslem, for he was once a Moslem when he was younger. Francis was like the Vicar of Bray. He changed his religion to suit his whims. When he realized that equipping Adah with birth-control gear would release her from the bondage of child-bearing, Francis went Catholic. When he started failing his examinations and was feeling very inferior to his fellow Nigerians, he became a Jehovah's Witness.

Adah now looked at the woman with the cherished baby with new eyes. She never stopped talking, she never stopped laughing. Her laughter was as loud as that of a man. She was rough, not as cultivated as the sleek, younger woman next to Adah. The sleek one in number eleven bed, though normally a very quiet girl, took it upon herself to talk to Adah all the time. It must have been very difficult for her, because she had not had her baby yet. It was a complicated case. She was weeks overdue, she told Adah. The surgeons and doctors did not know whether to operate or not. They were still waiting, including her husband. That husband of hers, tall, handsome, well-dressed and well-groomed, looked like the god Apollo. There must be something special about the man, because he came to see his wife at any time during the day. The nurses and doctors allowed him in. Even the surgeon that cut Adah up, who was another handsome dark man, white, but with that type of skin colouring white people usually have when they have stayed years and years in the sunshine, or that artificial tan which white women paint on themselves, to give them a healthy look. The surgeon's hair was thick, black and straight, his nose and mouth heavy like those of a Negro, but he was English, or so they claimed. And he was a great man. A man who knew how to handle his knife, a man who took a particular interest in all the patients he had operated on. He kept coming to see how Adah was getting on, night and day, during the first four days after the operation, when Adah was half-way between this world and the next one.

He, this surgeon that knew how to handle his knife well, did not do any preaching and sermonizing to Adah, about why she should try to live and all that, but he kept telling his white-coated disciples that few patients had died from his knife. And not only that, the scar always healed nicely, without disfiguring the woman. Adah liked this surgeon and his confidence, even when, on some of those nights, it seemed to everybody, even to Adah herself, that she was going to be one of the few patients he lost. The man's confidence never left him. So Adah started to believe with him that she was made for this world and not the next. Not yet anyway. The dark, handsome surgeon won. Adah lived, and became a living specimen in that ward.

Nobody called her by her actual name. She was saddled with several, just like titles. Some of her titles she could not help having, some were not necessary, others were bestowed on her by that unique baby she had. To the other women in the ward, she was Caesar; to the strings of young doctors who kept trailing in the wake of the surgeon, she was 'Cord presentation', whatever that meant. To the night nurses, she was the mother of Mohammed Ali, because her baby was loud-mouthed, troublesome and refused to be tamed. He would sleep all through the afternoon. If all other babies were crying their heads off, Bubu would sleep through. Their cries never disturbed him. But as soon as it was night, and other babies in the nursery decided to sleep, then Bubu would wake, and wake in style, loud and demanding. Of course, all the other babies would be woken up by his cries. So in the day, Bubu was very popular, but at night, he was a terror. In the end, a special emergency nursery was fitted out at the end of the corridor for him alone, and Adah was free to go and see him there. Bubu was given VIP treatment, right there in the hospital.

On the fourth day, they removed the tube that had sealed Adah's mouth.

Those four days were like four centuries to her. So she could now talk, but could not move about on her bed, and her back was sore. She did not mind that, for was not her mouth free at last?

She started pumping the sleek woman in number eleven with questions. How did she come to marry a man as hand-some as her husband? What did it feel like, marrying a man who was almost old enough to be your father? How did it feel to be loved and respected as she was, being showered with presents of flowers, funny dolls that made mad music, beautiful boxes tied with bright, beautiful ribbons and containing all sorts of things? One or two contained a funny jack-in-the-box. All different, doing different things. How did it feel to be treated with so much respect by the big, masculine-looking but rather motherly sister of the ward? In answer, the sleek woman simply smiled. She was used to being indulged, used to being spoiled, but she was a very simple person despite it all. She had been the big man's secretary. His wife had died years ago, leaving him with the two sons Adah had seen. Yes, Adah had seen them, tall like their father but too thin for Adah's liking. They needed to be fed more, Adah had thought. One was in a university, reading Law, the other was a partner in a certain firm, the sleek woman told Adah. Marrying their father was the greatest thing that had ever happened to her. She was an adopted daughter, she never knew who her real mother was or her father. She had tried, but failed, to find out whether her real parents were dead or alive. Her adoptive parents were good, she added quickly, too quickly for Adah, who could never guess how it could be possible for somebody else to love you as if you were their very own flesh and blood. They did love her, her adoptive parents, but she was determined to make a happy home for herself, where she would be loved, really loved, and where she would be free to love. She had been lucky. It seemed as if her dream was coming true.

'It is not coming true; it is true. You are now almost like a princess,' Adah said, wanting to cry.

Their conversation was interrupted by the arrival of the sleek woman's film-star-like husband. Adah's attention was diverted by the big surgeon and his group of six disciples. Adah, for once, did not want to see all these people. Doctor or no doctor, surgeon or no surgeon, why could not the man test her alone, without all those men with hungry eyes, like vultures, looking on?

They brought a flowered screen to give her a little privacy. She was sorry for this, because she liked to watch the way the sleek woman's husband usually sat by her bedside, taking her hand gently, both of them laughing quietly, sometimes just sitting there, he stroking her forehead, saying nothing, just sitting there, like lovers in the cheap movie pictures Adah had seen at home. You read about things like that, you saw actresses and actors acting things like that on the screen for money. It never occurred to Adah that such things could be real.

As soon as the big surgeon started to expose her to the view of those student doctors, or surgeons, or whatever title they were going to be called by when they qualified, Adah burst into tears. Why, what was the matter? asked the big man. They concluded that it was the after-baby blues. Adah would not stop. She did not want to stop because she might be tempted to babble the truth to them. She might be tempted to tell them for once in her whole life she hated being what she was. Why was it she could never be loved as an individual, the way the sleek woman was being loved, for what she was and not just because she could work and hand over her money like a docile child? Why was it that she was not blessed with a husband like that woman who had to wait for seventeen years for the arrival of her baby son? The whole world seemed so unequal, so unfair. Some people were created with all the good things ready-made for them, others were just created like mistakes. God's mistakes.

All Adah could see at that moment was the sleek girl being kissed and loved, and the woman who had to wait for seventeen years walking round the ward proudly with her child. She did not think of what life was like for a little girl who was aware that she was adopted; that the little girl might sometimes wonder whether her parents ever wanted her? That the little girl could sometimes feel unwanted even by her adoptive parents. As for the woman with the baby son, Adah could not imagine the aches and pains that went with those seventeen years.

She found it very difficult to control her tears even when she had stopped feeling antagonistic towards the big surgeon and his six disciples. They were waiting for her to stop. The Indian woman in the group looked as if she was being forced to eat shit. Her face looked ugly. She wanted to cry with Adah. Adah knew she was Indian because her sari was sweeping the ward floor under her white coat, and her long black hair was done up in a long single plait, dangling behind her back like a horse's tail which African chiefs used to ward off flies in public.

The surgeon made some sympathetic sounds, telling Adah not to worry. They would come again to talk to her. He whispered something to a nurse standing by. The disciples all smiled at Adah, sheepishly, the surgeon told her she was a good girl, for she was progressing very rapidly. They left her. None of them turned round to stare at her any more.

They just disappeared very quickly, like a group of silent, dumb people, whose tongues had been taken from their mouths.

The time for the visitors to rush into the wards had come. Adah was by the door. She could see anxious relatives clutching bunches of flowers and gifts, waiting impatiently for the big sister to say the word. These relatives were like children, waving anxiously at the mothers who, by then, had been tidied up by the brisk nurses. Most of the mothers had combed their hair, powdered their noses. They all had gay nightdresses on, they looked happy and expectant. Adah was happy for them, not because she was part of the picture, but because she was a good watcher. The only table that was bare in the whole ward was hers. She had no flowers, she had no cards. They had no friends, and Francis did not think flowers were necessary. Adah did not ask him why he did not buy her flowers; maybe he had not noticed that the other women had flowers. She did not blame him for this, because in Lagos few people bought flowers for new mothers. She would point it out, though, so that he would learn for the future. Maybe he would even buy her flowers for tomorrow, she thought. That would be a miracle though. Why was it that men took such a long time to change, to adapt, to reconcile themselves to new situations?

The woman in number eight was Greek, large and voluble. She had told Adah that she lived in Camden Town, that she had a little girl at home. The girl was the same age as Adah's Titi. But the woman was gorgeous. She had about ten housecoats all with beautiful frills and edgings. She was a seamstress, she said. She sewed for Marks and Spencer's, so she had a great many sub-standard clothes which the firm allowed her to keep. That evening, she was wearing a large nylon nightdress, with a satin bow in the front, tucked in nicely between her large breasts. She had let her hair down and it was held in place with the remnant of the satin material. She looked like a blue flower, sitting there, large, decorative, smiling and waving at her husband, who was still outside.

Adah started to worry about her nightdress. The nurses had kindly changed her into a cleaner one, but it was a hospital nightdress. They were like men's shirts, red-striped, with long shapeless sleeves and collars. The background of the material was pink, but the stripes stood out, just like red veins. Adah did not mind so much wearing the shirt-like nightdress, with the blood-coloured stripes. What she minded was that she was the only woman wearing one. All the others had their own nightdresses. She was going to tell Francis about it. She would ask him to buy her one from Marks and Spencer's. Her special nightdress that was coming from Marks and Spencer's would be blue too, like the Greek woman's. But she would tell Francis she did not want so many frills and tucks. They would make her look like an over-decorated Christmas tree and she would not like that. All she wanted was plain, straight blue nylon or Terylene, or anything, as long as it was soft, transparent and blue. She thought a bit about its transparency, and decided that Francis would not like that. He would accuse her of showing off to those doctors with the curious eyes and clinical smiles. No, she would not ask Francis to buy a transparent one, she would ask him to buy a double one that had something like a petticoat sewn inside. Those were very beautiful, because the petticoats were usually edged with lovely lace. Yes, that was the one she was going to tell Francis to buy her. She would not mind if he bought only one, because in a day or two she was sure she would get better and could sneak into the bathroom to wash her nightdress so that it would be nice and clean for the next day. But wouldn't Francis moan about the cost of the blue nightdress with the lacy petticoat? Wouldn't he accuse her of envying her neighbours, of wanting to keep up with the Joneses next door? What answer was she going to give?

She thought and thought again. Why, Francis had never given her a present. After all she had given him this Mohammed Ali of a son. After all, the son was going to carry his name, not hers, even though she was carrying the ugly Caesarean scars all her life. And what of the pain she was still going through? Yes, she deserved a present from Francis. She did not mind if he bought it with her money, but she was going to show it round the ward, and say to her sleek neighbour, 'Look, my husband bought me a double nightdress, with a lacy petticoat, just what I was dreaming about.' She was going to do that. Well, she was learning. When in Rome, do as Rome does. When in University College Hospital in Gower Street, do as they do in University College Hospital in Gower Street. Neat, that is.

The gong sounded. The visitors rushed in, laughing, clutching more flowers, more parcels, more presents. Adah was just getting ready to watch as usual, because Francis seldom came early, because of the children. That was all right with her because Francis did not kiss in public; he could hardly ask her how she was feeling, because to him Adah was always his and no illness, no god could take Adah from him, so why bother to ask how she was feeling, when he was sure she would get better anyway? So they usually had nothing to talk about. Adah could only ask and worry about Titi and Vicky. Vicky's face was beginning to accuse her. She told herself that it was a sure sign that she was getting better. A few days before, she was not even aware she had Titi or Vicky. She was not aware of anything, anything at all. So, Francis was not coming early and she was going to watch the crowd of happy relatives spoiling their women.

A nurse rushed in after the relatives. She was coming to Adah, with an uncertain smile on her face. It was a smile of embarrassment. She was behaving like somebody who has been entrusted with a nasty job. But she had to do this job nevertheless. She came to Adah, one hand holding her white cap, which looked as if it was falling off, and she was smiling this uncertain smile. She was talking to Adah, but her eyes were watching the visitors.

She said, her voice low and husky: 'Mrs Obi, you must tell your husband, when he comes, to bring you your night-dress because, you see, you are not really meant to wear the hospital gown after your baby has been born. You only wear them in the labour-room. But we thought that maybe you did not know.' She smiled again and then disappeared.

Adah noticed that she was the youngest of all the nurses. Why is it that the ugliest jobs are usually given to the young? Part of their training? Couldn't the ward sister have made a better job of telling her that she was not allowed to wear hospital dress in an open ward? Not to worry, it all came down to the same thing. Francis must buy her a nightdress.

But being told to do so in the way the young nurse did took the glamour off it. Now, it was imperative, it was a duty, an order which had to be obeyed. It would not be a present any more.

This left a hollow in her sore stomach.

She was now sure people were talking about her. *Look at that nigger woman with no flowers, no cards, no visitors, except her husband who usually comes five minutes before the closing time, looking as if he hates it all. Look at her, she doesn't have a nightdress of her own. Is she from Holloway, from a prison? Only patients from prison wear hospital dresses in the ward.* Adah was sure that the granny talking and gesticulating wildly about the bed of her granddaughter was talking about her not having a nightdress. She was sure the short stocky Greek man in a black coat, sitting rather uncomfortably in the straight-backed hospital chair was talking about her. All the conversation buzzing, buzzing around her, was about her. The buzzing went on and on, and would never stop. She could even hear her name being mentioned, especially by the Greek man. She did not want to hear any more. She did not want to think any more. She did not want to see any more. She closed her eyes, she dived into the sheets, covering herself up. The world would not see her now, the world would not know whether she had a hospital dress or her own dress. Had she not covered herself up, just like a dead person?

If the sleek woman, who was being talked to by her husband's two handsome sons, had noticed that Adah was doing something funny, she did not think it important enough to embarrass her visitors with it. If one or two visiting relatives had thought to themselves that it was odd, her diving in among the sheets like that, they would have shrugged their shoulders and said to themselves, one can never tell with these blacks, they sometimes behave as if they have their minds in their arses.

Adah was grateful to them all for not asking her what she was up to. She wanted some privacy, and the only one available at the time was under the sheets.

She told Francis she was not asleep, because on arrival his first question was about why she was lying there like that, covering her head up. Then he smiled, he had good news for her. Had he not told her over and over again that she was a wife in a million? Was that not why he was trying to keep her away from their prying neighbours and friends, because if they knew how helpful she was they might grow jealous? He was very lucky to have her.

Adah wondered what the good news was that was making Francis look so pleased with himself. Had he got himself a big job or something? No, Francis was not the type of man who would go and look for a job unless pushed to it. He was the type of person who believed the world owed him so much that he need not put anything back. Nothing, not even an earthquake, could change that crystallized core in Francis. That was the only good news that could make Adah happy in her present emotional state. Coming to have her baby in this hospital had opened her eyes a good deal. Why, many English men took home their wives' nightdresses to wash them. She was determined to try it all on Francis. She was going to ask him to buy the nightdresses, not one any more, but two or even three, and she was going to ask him to wash them when they were soiled; after all, the soiling would be due to the losses she was going through because of the son she had had for him. The son that would bear his name like a banner. But first the good news, then the argument later.

'Now why don't you tell me the good news?' she asked, smiling as much as her sewn-up stomach would allow her. 'Tell me, I am dying to hear it.'

'First read this,' Francis commanded. He handed her a letter from her boss at the library where she was working. The woman, her boss, God bless her, advised her to make the best of her stay in hospital and give herself some rest. Adah was trying to read and concentrate, but Francis was impatient and was urging her on to get to the last paragraph, which he said was the most important. Adah skipped most of the middle part of the letter just to satisfy Francis, and read the last part. Yes, it was good news in a way. The Finchley Borough had decided to pay her a lump sum for the holidays she had not taken. Her boss remarked that she hoped Adah would use this money to take a holiday after the confinement and get some clothes for herself. She concluded the letter by telling her that the staff had collected some money and bought her a red woollen cardigan to go with the *lappa* with birds on it that she usually wore to work.

'They are very kind people in that library. I hope they will take me back after all this. I must go and thank them personally some time,' Adah remarked smiling and thinking that God had helped her so much with this small fortune. So she could now tell Francis about the nightdress which the nurse wanted her to have, she could now afford to buy the double ones, and she was going to buy two or three . . . but Francis was talking, about something he said was very important. Adah forced her mind back to what he was saying.

'. . . you know that course Mr Ibiam said had helped him in passing his Cost and Works accountancy examinations? I can now afford to pay for it. It costs less than forty pounds, and that would hasten my success. I am paying for the whole course on Monday, so that the whole lot can be sent to me as soon as possible.'

What does one say to such a man? That he is an idiot? That he is selfish? That he is a rogue? Or a murderer? Nothing Adah could think of could convey her feelings adequately. She simply sighed and, instead, asked about the children, whom Francis seemed to have forgotten to mention. She was told they were well and that they did not miss her much.

'Don't they? Suppose I had died a few days ago, who would have taken care of them? Tell me. With you still living in your dreams about what you are going to be in the future and what you are going to be in the New Kingdom of God. But you forget the children need you now. I don't care whether you become a Nkrumah or another Zik. I want a husband now and a father for my children now!' Adah cried.

Francis looked about him wildly. He was sure they could not be heard by the rest of the patients and their visitors, but Adah was speaking in their Ibo language and that meant gesticulating in the air.. The gesticulations were wild, like the arms of a windmill that had gone mad. She kept her voice low, but was talking and talking and would never stop.

'If you are worried about who is going to look after the

children, if you had died, well, I'll tell you this. My mother brought us all up and I don't see . . .'

'If you don't go out of this ward, or stop talking, I shall throw this milk jug at you. I hate you now, Francis, and one day I shall leave you. I did not bring my children into the world to be brought up by a woman who can't even sign her name. A woman who used her thumb on our marriage certificate because she could not write. If you really want to know, I brought my children here to save them from the clutches of your family, and, God help me, they are going back as different people; never, never, are they going to be the type of person you are. My sons will learn to treat their wives as people, individuals, not like goats that have been taught to talk. My daughters . . . God help me, nobody is going to pay any bleeding price for them. They will marry because they love and respect their men, not because they are looking for the highest bidder or because they are looking for a home . . .'

At the mention of a home, Adah started to cry. If only she had had a home, she would not have married so early. If only Papa had not died when he did. If only her people in Lagos had been civilized enough to know that a girl who decided to live by herself and study for her degree was not necessarily a prostitute, if only . . . Her thoughts went on and on. Now here she was in a foreign country, with no single friend, except her children . . .

Yes, I have my children. They are only babies, but babies become people, men and women. I can switch my love to them. Leave this person. No, live with him as long as it is convenient. No longer. Adah dried her tears. Crying showed softness and weakness. Crying was too late now. There was no Ma and no Pa. And her brother Boy was miles away, and could not be of any help. She had to act for herself. She was looking for a home. She had never had one since Pa died years ago; she had looked for it in the wrong place and among the wrong people. That did not mean the whole world was wrong or that she could never start another home, now that she had her babies to share it with. She smiled at Francis, thanking God for giving her him as a tool with which it was possible to have her children. She would not harm him, because he was the father of her babies. But he was a dangerous man to live with. Like all such men, he needed victims. Adah was not going to be a willing victim.

She smiled again. She told him that the hospital authorities wanted her to buy a nightdress. She said she would like to have blue, but the look on Francis's face and her former outburst had sapped all her energy. She did not have the courage to tell him she would need more than one, because she was still losing blood heavily, she could not tell him she would like a beautiful and fashionable one. Adah suddenly realized that she was not dealing with the husband of her dreams, but with an enemy. She had to be very careful, otherwise she would get hurt. She did not care any more about flowers or cards, but wanted only to get well quickly and go back to her children.

'Suppose this money had not arrived, what would you have bought the nightdress with?'

There was no need to reply. Her pay for the month had just arrived, the letter said so; they could afford several nightdresses, if Francis did not think them a wasteful luxury. But she said nothing. Instead, she turned her head to the rest of the patients, got bored with watching, closed her eyes and went to sleep.

Two days later, the nightdress did arrive. It was blue. The shape and cut was exactly like the one Adah had in the hospital. It was just a long cotton shirt, the type specially made for the very old. Adah was indifferent. At least she would not feel guilty about wearing the hospital's shirt any more.

She did not bother to show it round as she had planned, because she was not proud of it. It was not beautiful, and she could only have one. So for the rest of her stay she learned another rule. She should keep to herself. If she got herself involved in any kind of gossip or conversation, she might be lured to talk about herself, about her children and about her husband. She did not want to do that any more. There was nothing to talk about.

Soon the women in the ward started going home. Everybody was anxious to be home before Christmas. The sleek lady was the first to melt away unobtrusively. She had to go

134

to another ward, she told Adah. She wished her luck during her stay in England and told her it had been nice knowing her and that she hoped Adah got better soon. Adah was so moved that she was tempted to act just as she would have in Nigeria. She wanted to ask the lady for her address, but something in the lady's politeness stopped her. It was the type of politeness one usually associated with high intelligence. She could talk to Adah in the hospital ward, she could joke with her, she could tell her the story of her life, because she knew they would never meet again, not on this earth. So, Adah just thanked her and wished her luck. She slipped out of the ward, padding noiselessly, so that people who saw her thought she was simply going for a bath. But she was gone. She died a few days afterwards. Nobody told the few remaining mothers the details. All they knew was that she had died. The nurses would reveal no more.

Adah wanted to go home.

Getting ready for home was another ordeal. You dressed yourself and your new baby in its brand new clothes and new shawl. Then the baby would be shown round in his first civilian clothes, and everybody would coo and remark on how smart he looked. They would also congratulate the mother on her trim figure. These congratulations were not always very sincere, because all new mothers went home with that frontal bulge which disappears only with time. But on that day, the day the mothers leave the hospital, they would squeeze and stuff themselves into tight dresses or suits. One could watch these women with sympathy, trying to prove to themselves that nothing had changed, that they had not lost their figures, that they were still trim and nice, just as they were before their babies were conceived; that having the babies did not mean losing their youth and that, like every young woman in the street, they could go about in ordinary clothes and not the tent-like outfits which had been their lot over the past months.

Adah's African costume solved the figure problem for her. Her Ibo *lappa* would stretch and stretch so that there was no need for her to draw her tummy in. Her *lappa* would cover it all for her. She had asked Francis to bring her the one with 'Nigerian Independence, 1960' written all over it. She was going to show people that she came from Nigeria and that Nigeria was an independent republic. Not that the other women did not know, but Adah felt that she would like them to remember it always, that she came from Nigeria, and that Nigeria was independent.

Her problem was the baby's clothes. When she had had Vicky, the Americans had been so good to her, ordering all her baby's clothes from Washington. The shawls and the baby's blankets were all very soft and beautiful. But now, Adah had had to use them twice over. She did not mind the blankets and the baby's clothes, what she minded about was the shawl. It had gone off-white. It was never really white when it was new, but had had that sort of beautiful baby-soft creamy whiteness. Now after nursing Vicky with it and after about a hundred washes, that creaminess had lost its softness. It had now got that type of creaminess one could not quickly dissociate with dirt, bad washing and poverty. Surely every new child deserved a new first outfit. She could not tell her worries to her husband, because she knew the answer she would get. He would tell her that a shawl was a shawl and that was that. The agony Adah went through just for that creamy shawl! Could she just disappear from the ward with her baby, whilst the other mothers were sleeping, so that they would not notice how shabbily her baby was dressed? Should she tell the nurse not to show her baby round because she did not like him being displayed like that? What was she going to do? The nightdress episode had made her quiet, uncommunicative even to the Greek woman opposite her. But the trouble was that Adah guessed people knew why she had so suddenly gone quiet. If only she could be confident enough to put on a show of indifference, that would have made life much more simple for her friends in the ward and for herself too. But this type of attitude, that of the sophisticated poor, was to be achieved much later. On that December day, to twenty-year-old Adah, a new shawl was the end of the world. Since she did not have it, she was beginning to envy the sleek lady who had escaped it all by dying. If only she had died, if only the nurses did not think her baby gorgeous, because he had thick curly hair, when most babies in the nursery were bald, if only they would simply let her grab him and disappear.

Francis came with her *lappa.* Adah tied it round herself
hurriedly, but refused to go back to the ward. She stood firm
in the hospital corridor. She watched the nurse showing
Bubu around, she was sure the nurse was taking a long time
in doing that just because Bubu's shawl was old. She was sure
that the women were all laughing at her and saying 'poor
nigger!' She stood there, biting her nails, almost eating her
own flesh in anxiety. *Give me my baby back,* her heart cried
painfully. But the nurse was showing them all, the women, the
doctors, anybody who happened to be around, that this was
their special baby, born miraculously, for whom the mother
had suffered so. And was he not worth all the sufferings and
sacrifices? It was Francis who followed the nurse, listening
to all the talk. Of course he heard only the sweet words, he
did not see that the baby's shawl was not new. That it was
off-white and not soft. Men are so blind.

In the taxi that was speeding her home to Vicky and Titi,
she wondered if the nurse could be really sincere? Did those
women in the ward really admire her baby or were they
just curious to see what a new African baby looked like? Suppose one or two were really serious, sincerely admiring her
Bubu, should she not have gone round to say a nice good-bye
to them?

She started to feel guilty. She had thought only of herself
all the time and not those women who were doing their best
to be friendly. What was happening to her? At school,
she was never really happy, but she did not have this suspicious attitude towards other people. She tried to find the
answer, but the only anchor she could find was her relationship with her parents-in-law, and Francis. She knew she was
not loved, and was being used to give Francis an education
which the family could not afford. Why should she blame them
then? Had she loved Francis to start with? She had only
begun to love and care for him later. But the love was short-
lived because Francis did nothing to keep it alive. She felt
she was being betrayed, by the very man she had begun to
love. Was that what love meant? This pain? She so wished
she could tell her worries to someone. She wished Pa was
alive. Pa would have understood. Since there was no one to

137

tell, she had to put on a cloak of indifference. Francis could now do what he liked, she was not going to tell him what to do. She would only protest if his behaviour started to affect her children. Was it this betrayal of Francis and his people that made her suspicious of the women in the ward?

She wished, now, that she had said good-bye, nicely. But it was too late. Even if she went back tomorrow, one or two would have gone. She could never get that very same group of people, in the same ward having their babies, again. It could never be repeated. She had lost the opportunity of saying good-bye nicely. The only good thing she had learned was that she would never let such a thing happen to her in the future. She must learn to thank people, even for their smiles, and kindly nods.

This consoling conclusion, this new code of conduct Adah learned from the hospital and from staying together with other women for thirteen days, was to be with her for a long time. She now looked forward to seeing her children, whom she was going to love and protect. To her children, the indifferent attitude would never apply. You see, they were her children, and that made all the difference.

The taxi stopped in front of the house in Willes Road, and she scooped her babies into her arms. They were alive and well. They had not forgotten who she was.

10 Applying the Rules

It was a very cold winter that year. Before it started to snow, the air was biting, the atmosphere grey and thick with fog. On some days, you could hardly see beyond a few feet in front of you, so thick was the fog. Then the snow started to fall. It fell and fell as if it would never stop. It was thick on the ground, thick on the roofs of the houses, thick in the air, falling, falling all the time. The ground seemed to have all gone white, never to change to any other colour.

Adah was lucky. She and her family cooked in the same room that served as living-room, bedroom, lounge, bathroom. The only thing they had outside this room was the lavatory.

The children seldom went out. There was no place in which they could play, so the same room served them as the play-room as well. Titi accepted their baby brother with a shy smile, saying, 'It's a baby, that!' Adah agreed with her that Bubu was a baby. Vicky looked and looked at this new baby that was inheriting his old cot, and did not really know what to make of it all. He would stand there by the cot, peering between the railings and tell his mother that the baby 'is clying'.

Francis went to work for two weeks. Adah felt very guilty about this. She knew her man ought to go out to work for their living, but in her own particular family she had been doing all the work. It seemed to her that she was failing, by staying at home and letting Francis go out to work in that terrible winter. Francis would worsen the effect when he came home, telling her how very difficult it was to work as a postman in England during Christmas. 'You are given a big bag of letters and parcels as heavy as the load of Christian in *The Pilgrim's Progress*. And, like Christian, you are expected to carry the load, up the stairs leading into flats, and down the stairs to those living in basements.' The load on his back was heavy, the work was killing, going up and down like a mad yo-yo. The work was humiliating, treading the streets with the bag on your back, your nose running into your mouth, and worst of all, you were given a black band for your arm, as if you had lost your mother or something. Adah would shudder at this recital and feel awful, wishing she was well enough to go back to her job to save her husband all this pain. The most frightful part of the whole business of Post Office jobs during Christmas was the English dogs. Those people, the English, they did worship their dogs! Adah gave a nod. Was that not the reason why they had a saying in their own language that you should love them and love their dogs? They love dogs, the English do. Yes, they love their dogs, Francis continued, so much so that they would rather the dogs butcher a black man, than let the black man kill the dog. Adah considered this, and decided that it was not fair that people should let their dogs butcher a black man. After all, the black man was only a postman, delivering Christmas cards and parcels. Had it ever actually happened, Adah wondered, or was Francis thinking it could happen and happen to him? She asked him this. Francis was sure not only that it could happen, but that it was going to happen to him. And he was sure he had heard somewhere that it had happened to a man he used to know. Adah did not want to ask where he heard it and what the name of the man was, because Francis might accuse her of wanting to know too much.

But the picture Francis conjured up in her mind clung like a leech. She had seen the picture of the man Christian, dressed shabbily like Robinson Crusoe, climbing a steep hill with a staff in his hand, puffing and puffing. So that was how Francis would look, the big load on his back, puffing up and down the stairs; and then, all of a sudden, the mad English dogs would chase him, barking like mad, hungry to butcher him, to eat him up, and their owners would be standing there laughing and saying 'poor nigger'! This thought would send a chilling feeling through her veins and she would shudder at it. The thought of Francis running, running for his life and the dogs in hot pursuit. The picture would not go away. It stayed there with her, so much so that when Francis left for the Post Office in the mornings she would say to herself,

'I may never see him again. The dogs may have eaten him up by the evening.' But Francis usually turned up, ready to recite more horrid experiences. It was brutal of Shakespeare to say that 'Cowards die many times before their deaths', because the cowards really suffer. What they imagine is so real to them that they actually suffer. Adah had never died before, and she had not been fortunate enough to see somebody who had died and then come back to tell her what it was like, but she had suffered the fear of death, and had seen Francis suffer the fear of being eaten up by the angry English dogs, so she knew that this fear could be real. Really painful fear.

She took Titi to a play-group at Lindhurst Hall, just round the corner from Willes Road, next to Athlone Street Library. Normally it took her only five minutes or so to cover this short distance, but it was winter and there was snow on the ground and it was her first day of using her feet after the cutting-up in the hospital. Her feet were reluctant to obey her. It seemed to her as if she had to learn to walk all over again. She held Titi, now three, tightly, but Titi was so happy at the thought of escaping from their one-room mansion that she skipped up and down, down and up, on the dangerous snow. Adah let her go, her feet wobbling, her head light, and her vision blurred. It seemed to her that she was seeing lots and lots of colourful balloons in the air, blue, red, and yellow, but there was more blue than the other colours. So she walked with caution, taking her time. So this was what the sister of the ward was talking about when she said she was sure Adah was not well enough to look after three young children. Yes, the sister was right. She was not well enough.

Anger welled up inside her. Was she so ill without knowing it, and Francis telling her the story of the dogs that would eat him up, and she blaming herself for letting her husband work? Anger mixed with her fear. Suppose it was going to be like this till the end of her days? Suppose she was going to remain a weakling, with wobbly feet, and eyes that would not focus, and a brain that went round and round like the ripples in a pool. What would she do then? How would she study to be a librarian and then a writer, which she was sure she was going to be by the time she was forty? Let the dogs eat Francis up, she could not care less. She started to blame herself for worrying about it in the first place. All men do work, why should he want to be different? Had Adah not learned that in the hospital? Had she forgotten her resolution, the one she made then, that she was going to be indifferent to Francis's worries? Here she was five days after leaving the hospital, worrying about it all, forgetting everything she had learned.

When she got to the play-group, the woman who was running it congratulated her on the birth of her baby, but remarked that she looked tired. She should not have come. She would return Titi to her, at noon, when the play-group closed. She would collect Titi in the mornings on her way in until Adah was really strong. Did she not realize that she had lost a lot of weight? She was surprised the hospital had discharged her so soon, she should have stayed longer, the kind woman observed as she made Adah a nice hot mug of tea.

On her way home, Adah saw another student carrying a big bag, but she seemed to be walking very, very briskly, almost as if she was happy working for Christmas. She was a woman. And she was black.

Adah leaned against the dirty supports of the overhead bridge off Carltoun Street, watching this young woman clip-clapping the letter-boxes as she went along. Adah thought she could hear her singing. Wasn't she aware of the dogs, the weight of the bag, the black band and all that? Adah shrugged her tired shoulders, picking her way back to Willes Road with care. When she came to the front of the café run by the Greek woman and her baldy husband, she rested again, savouring the smell of bacon and chips coming from the café. At last she got home, and slept most of the day.

Francis came back in the evening, telling her that he covered the worst houses ever built in England. He was sure those houses were specially built to torment him. Did Adah not know that those houses had their letter-boxes on their roofs? Adah said, 'Huh!' and Francis said that 'roof' was just a figure of speech. But that the letter-boxes were almost on the roofs, because he had to stretch and stretch to reach them.

Adah listened, and yawned on purpose. Francis's words did not cling this time. They went in through one ear, and came out of the other, without leaving a single scratch on her. That did not stop Francis, for he loved the sound of his own voice.

Christmas came and that particular Christmas, Adah was happy to tell people that her husband was a Jehovah's Witness, because there was no money for any celebration.

Mrs Noble gaped at this piece of news and asked, 'You mean, you're not buying any presents for your children, not even a single toy?'

Adah said, no, they were not buying because you see, Jehovah's Witnesses believed that Jesus was born in October and that the Christmas celebrations were the work of the devil. The devil had turned people away from God, and people celebrated for the devil at Christmas instead of for Jesus in October. Mrs Noble sighed, trying to follow Adah's reasoning and came up with another piercing question. She was an inquisitive woman, that Mrs Noble.

She asked, 'I did not see you celebrate anything here last October or did you?'

'No, we did not,' Adah replied and wondered why the Witnesses don't celebrate in October; maybe because they think the birth of Christ was not important enough to bother with.

Adah did not really care. She believed that there was a man upstairs who cared for what happened to everybody, including herself and her children. She knew there was a man called Jesus. But the part of Christianity that still confused her was why this great man should be called the son of God. Adah did not want to ask anybody about this, because they might think her stupid, not knowing why Jesus was the son of God, so she started celebrating His birth because she was born into it. Her Pa had liked to preach in the church on Sundays and she had been a choir girl ever since she could remember. Then she had taught children at Sunday school at All Saints' Church in Yaba, in Lagos. How, then, could she go to a vicar and say, please, Mr Vicar, I still don't understand why you call Jesus the son of God because His birth was so unorthodox? Adah did not mind celebrating His birth because, from what He said and did, He was a great poet, a great philosopher, a great politician and a great psychologist, all in one. The world celebrated the births of lesser men, why then should she grudge this great man the celebration of His birth? And what did it matter whether it was celebrated in October or December? If we humans could rationalize about dates and all that, she believed that God, who made the humans who could rationalize and come to terms with things, would be able to rationalize still more. So, having equipped herself with this idea, she did not share Mrs Noble's distress. The long and short of it was that she had no money for Christmas; God would understand.

God did understand and comforted her a little. Because, all of a sudden, a big parcel arrived as if it were from Santa Claus. It was from the kind woman who was her boss at the North Finchley Library. There was a doll with eyes that blinked, dressed in white lace with white shoes and socks to match, for Titi. There was a little guitar for Vicky and a hopping, squeaking hedgehog for Bubu. They were so lovely that Adah could hardly wait for Christmas Day to give them to her children. That was the only thing that had worried her, her children having no toys, when every child had one at Christmas. The Nobles made the situation worse. There was this man who was a salesman, selling from door to door. From him, the Nobles bought a big doll as big as a child of two, a big pram, big enough to take a real baby, and all sorts of things for their five children. The cost of it all was so outrageous that Adah called upon Jesus to have mercy on them all. Then Mrs Noble explained to her that they were buying them on the 'never-never'. Adah did not know what the 'never-never' was and she looked so blank that Mrs Noble laughed, twisting her long red hair between her fingers.

Mr Noble then told her that here in England it was possible to buy many things without having a penny. You simply had to agree with the seller that you would pay every week, or every month as the case may be, and then you signed a paper or two, to say that you were sane and of sound mind and that you knew what you were doing when you promised to pay and all that; you then took the goods, just like that.

144

touching this and touching that, asking for the prices, and making her own selections, just like other mothers, bustling and rushing about in their Christmas busyness. Adah would have liked that, especially when she realized that, in England, Christmas is celebrated more in the shops than in the churches. As for her children, were they not too small, too isolated from other children to be able to compare notes and find out what they were missing?

The 24th was cold. For the first time in Adah's life she had to spend Christmas Eve indoors. It was cold and damp, and there was the white snow. There was not a single masquerade, no fireworks, no bell-ringing; it was all quiet, just as if Jesus had died, not like the celebration of His birth.

Francis went down to the Nobles to watch their television, because there were going to be some special Christmas films on the BBC channel. Adah had to stay with her babies, putting them to bed, telling them to be good and go straight to sleep, because there was going to be a big surprise for them the following day. She felt so lighthearted that she sang to her children '*Adeste Fideles*', and Titi, who seemed to have heard the tune somewhere before, joined in. Vicky looked at his mother and sister, his little Francis mouth pouting, his sleepy eyes wandering from one to the other, wondering what it was all about. Adah noticed that one of his ears seemed to move with the song, or was it her imagination? She touched the ear, but the child did not make any sound. Yes, there was something funny with that ear, it was definitely bigger than the other one, hanging down like an elephant's ear. Adah stopped singing. Funny, she had never noticed that one of Vicky's ears was bigger than the other one. It must have been natural, otherwise he would have winced with pain when she touched it. She ought to do something about it though, now that she had discovered the difference. It was shame for God to make a simple mistake like that, allowing one ear to be bigger than the other one. She could not correct it now; it was too late, it was too fixed. So she picked up a jar of Vaseline, which she bought for the baby's bottom, and rubbed it liberally in Vicky's big ear. Whether that was intended to ease the non-existent pain, or to correct the defect, or to ease her own mind, Adah did not know. But she felt

'Just like that?' Adah said unbelieving.

'Yes, just like that,' Pa Noble agreed.

Adah's mind sped back to Lagos. If a salesman could be stupid enough to allow people to buy on their doorsteps goods worth almost a hundred pounds, just like that, the salesman would soon have to close up his business. In Lagos, people would not pay, and if the salesman's demands became too irritating, people would just disappear. Then she asked Pa Noble: 'Suppose I run away, taking all his goods with me. What will he do then?'

'Ah,' Pa Noble laughed, 'you're thinking of home. Where will you run to here with all your children? It is not all that easy to find a new place to live, and people here usually leave a forwarding address. It is not easy to cheat here, because you'll be caught in the end.'

Adah did not need Pa Noble to tell her how difficult it was to find a house to live in, because she had experienced it. So the Nobles were going to pay every penny for what they were buying.

'But it will take a long time before you finish paying for all this.'

Pa Noble agreed again, but told Adah that in England you worshipped two goddesses; one is Christmas, the other one is holidays. As soon as they finished advertising for Christmas on television and in the papers, the next big thing is the annual holiday. So he was sure they would finish paying before they started saving for their holidays. He ended up by suggesting that Adah should get some toys for her children since she was not a Jehovah's Witness like her husband.

She was tempted to buy one or two small toys for pound or two and to lie to Francis that somebody had give them to the children, but how was she going to pay? From th two pounds a week housekeeping money Francis allowed he No, she would rather spend more on food and make with the presents sent by Mrs Konrad. In fact she was 'making do'; the presents would do all right. They were n they were beautiful and they were appropriate. Why w for more? She knew why, though: because she wante buy them herself, not from the never-never man, but t to Woolworth's or the other toy shops, browse ar better, having done something about the ear. Then she went to sleep.

Christmas morning was like any other morning, except that there was so much silence in the street. Snow had fallen in the night and there were no footmarks at all to smear the carpet of white. It was so silent, so peaceful, that Adah understood now why the carol 'Silent Night' belongs to that time of the year. In England it was silent night, holy night. In Nigeria it was noisy night, holy maybe, but fireworks night, the night of loud rejoicing, the night of palm-wine drinking in the streets, the night of bell-ringing. In England it was a hush, hush morning for was Jesus not lying asleep in the manger?

Mrs Noble had invited the children down for tea. She had made all sorts of elaborate preparations. There were jellies of different colours in a riot of Ali-Baba-shaped paper cups and paper plates and paper napkins. She had her room decorated in Christmas paper, all shining and bright. She bought paper hats to match the colours of the jellies she had made. Adah saw all the colours and thought it was a shame they had to be eaten. What were the colourings for? To make food more appetizing? To make it more beautiful? For it was beautiful. She hoped her children would enjoy it. As for her, the whole affair was too sugary. She was brought up with that taste; anything sugary tasted like cough medicine to her.

Adah got the children ready for Mrs Noble's tea party. She told Titi to eat everything on her plate, because Mrs Noble would be very angry if she made a mess of her food. Titi understood some of the reasoning Adah was trying to pump into her. That was all Adah could do and then hope for the best. It puzzled her, though, why people should be forced to eat everything that was set before them. In Nigeria the situation seldom arose. You finished all the food quickly and wanted some more, especially when you were a child. But here you had so much to start with that food became a bore. She knew that though she might never have enough money for other things, she would never allow her children to go hungry. There was no room for that.

She cleaned Titi and put on her red dress with spotty

147

pockets, which Adah had bought from one of the shops along Finchley Road. The dress had been too big for Titi, but Adah hemmed it up to size because she did not know if she could afford another dress like that for a long time. She sat Titi down in the middle of the bed, and told her to stay quiet and still so as not to mess up her new white tights. She then proceeded to Vicky. Then she saw the ear again. It was hanging down more than ever, it was getting bigger and bigger, there was no doubt about it. To cap it all Vicky was sitting down quietly, too quiet for Adah's Vicky. Panic took hold of her. Was Vicky sick again? Was the meningitis, or whatever the illness was called, coming back again? Was this another type of the same illness back to visit them again, and on Christmas Day? She did the only thing that came into her head. She yelled for Francis, who, as usual, was downstairs watching the Nobles' television.

Francis came up almost immediately because, unlike Mrs Noble, Adah seldom called her husband for anything. In fact, sometimes she was grateful to the Nobles for accommodating him for so long, because otherwise it would have meant his staying in the same room, getting in Adah's way, telling her she ought to have done this instead of that.

He came to ask her what it was that made her call him like that when she knew that he was watching a pantomime on television. She then told him that Vicky's right ear was getting as big as that of an elephant. Adah was sure that it was going to be bigger than an elephant's before morning, because it had grown bigger since the day before. Francis examined the ear and decided they had to call a doctor.

'A doctor on Christmas Day? He will not come and Vicky will die. Trust this child to be ill on a day when there is no doctor available!' Adah cried.

'Look, doctors are supposed to call on you at any time you're ill. It is the law,' Francis explained as he struggled into his coat, on his way to the telephone kiosk. 'I must call him out. Christmas or no Christmas, Vicky is ill and that's that.'

'But it is Christmas,' Adah persisted. 'At home in Nigeria you can't get a doctor out on Christmas Day, unless you are a millionaire or something.'

'Well, it is different here. You can get one on Christmas Day!'

With that announcement, Francis walked out, jingling the coins he was going to drop into the telephone slot in his hand.

Fancy getting somebody out in this weather and on this day, just because a child was ill. She guessed it was their right, but maybe this was a right that could be easily explained away, because they were blacks and because Vicky was only a baby and because it was Christmas Day. If anything should happen to Vicky now, Society would forgive the doctor, because he was a black child and had been taken ill on Christmas Day. Why then should Adah expect a doctor to call? She started to panic. She did not know what she was doing any more. Vicky was dying now. Had this enlarged ear not proved it? She dressed him in his best suit, the one she had kept for Mrs Noble's Christmas party. Even if it was going to be the last suit Vicky was ever going to wear in his life, it was going to be a good one. She touched the ear; it was getting hot as well. Adah knew it, death was coming, and on Christmas Day.

She was woken up from her terrible thoughts by a loud argument going on in the street below. She peeped through their dewy window and saw Francis and two policemen. God have mercy, what had Francis done now? They are taking him to jail, and he had come to say good-bye to them. Vicky was dying and she had to take care of the remaining children all by herself, with her wobbly feet that had refused to get strong and her eyes that kept seeing blue and yellow balloons all mixed up. She could not go downstairs, because she knew she would fall and break her neck and then the remaining children would have no one. She would stay put.

The noise was coming up the stairs. Francis was talking, shouting, explaining, talking and talking. The two policemen saw Vicky's ear, and agreed with Francis that it was growing much more rapidly than the rest of his body. Yes, he had to see a doctor.

Adah could not walk. Her eyes were going round and round, and would not focus. Would somebody explain to her what it was that was causing all this hullabaloo? It could not have been just because Vicky was ill. Had Francis in his present mood murdered the doctor?

Then one of the policemen spoke in a cool voice. He sounded like somebody with lots and lots of reasoning who was capable of using that reasoning when everybody around him was going mad. The policeman was tall and had a moustache and he was now telling them that a doctor would come; not their Indian doctor, because it was Christmas Day, but another one, the Indian one's locum. He would come and tell them what it was that was the matter with Vicky's ear.

But why the police? Adah wondered furiously. She could not ask anybody until the two police officers had gone. Then Francis started swearing and sending a man to his Maker and calling the man a bastard. Adah intervened and asked him who it was that had annoyed him so much.

'The bleeding Indian man. Do you know the stupid man thinks he is white? He is as black as the devil!' Then Francis thought again, walking up and down their one room. 'Do you know that he is as ugly as hell?'

Well, all that seemed logical to Adah. If the man was black as the devil, it followed that he would be as ugly as hell. What did Francis want? To put a man as handsome as Apollo in an ugly hell? That would not make sense. But what had the doctor done? Adah wanted to ask if only she was given the chance, but she was not because Francis was holding forth about the ethics of Medicine. Adah came to the conclusion that that husband of hers would have made a good doctor, knowing all the rules.

Then a black car pulled up in front of their house. A man, a very short man, young, not Indian but Chinese, came out. He was carrying a black bag. He must be the doctor. Adah rushed Vicky into their only bed, shoes, suit and all and asked him to stay there. She removed the rice she was boiling from the stove and would have poured it into the bin, if it had not been for Francis, who asked her whether she was going crazy. The man coming was a Chinaman. Did she not see his eyes and the shape of his round head like that of a calabash they used at home in Nigeria? Why then should she panic? The man, doctor or no doctor, was a second-class citizen too and could not come to show them any superior airs. This did not help Adah much, but it was nice to hear it.

The man came in, and was sorry for Adah and Francis for having such a terrible time on Christmas Day. He unpacked his instruments, and started to examine Vicky, pressing the ear all the time. Vicky followed his movements, fascinated. The boy was not in pain. His temperature was normal. The ear was now very big and warm, but that was all. The doctor sat down on the chair Adah gave him. His sharp Chinese eyes roamed round the room. He seemed to be scratching his bottom, but was doing it very gently. He was a Chinese, but one of those Chinamen who were either born in England or who had come here as children. He got up from his chair, scratching all the time, and then asked a funny question.

'Have you any bugs here? You know, bed-bugs?'

Adah prayed for the ground to swallow her up.

The doctor wrote a letter which she and Francis were to take to their doctor. The doctor, the Chinese one, noticed their discomfiture, and said, 'My grandmother in China used to kill bugs this way.' The doctor spread his well-kept hands wide in gesticulation. 'She used to get cigarette tins, and put all the feet of the bed in them, so that the bugs would fall into the tins, which had already been half-filled with water.' He took his leave, and the two stupid-looking parents told him how sorry they were, getting him out from his Christmas turkey. And the Chinaman told them not to worry, because children had a way of scaring parents so. How were they supposed to know that Vicky was not dying, but only bitten by a bed-bug?

It was nice of him to say so, but he went leaving a nasty pit in their stomachs. In desperation, Francis tore up the letter which they were supposed to give to their Indian doctor down the Crescent. The doctor had written exactly what he thought, that Vicky had been bitten by a bug.

'If only you did not have to add so much drama to it all. Why in the name of all the saints did you have to go to the police?'

'The Indian doctor would not come. He said it was his rest

day and I know that doctors are supposed to attend their
patients in an emergency. Why should he refuse to attend
to Vicky? And how was I supposed to know that he was
not seriously ill, and that he was only bitten by the bugs in
Pa Noble's house?'

There was nothing Adah could say. She herself was frightened, too, but she had known their own doctor would not
come. Though, after all, a doctor had come, and given them
a prescription, though it was very unorthodox.

At least some of the provisions of the Welfare State
worked for both second- and first-class citizens alike. Had
Francis not proved it by going to the police station when
the Indian doctor would not come? Adah wondered what
Francis would have done if it had all happened in Lagos.

After all that, there was not much left of the Christmas.
They ate their boiled rice, and Mrs Noble brought the left-
over jellies to Vicky. Vicky refused to eat them; he had never
seen food look so colourful.

11 Population Control

The snow melted from the pavements, from the gardens
and from the roofs of the houses. Spring was in the air and
everything sprung up as if injected with new life by the
gods. Even in a dark street, as dark as Willes Road in Kentish
Town, one could hear the birds sing.

One Monday morning, when her family were still asleep,
Adah got together her wash things to have her bath. There
was no bathroom in the house in which they lived so she
paid visits to the public baths in Prince of Wales Road several
times in the week. It was on one of these visits, on a Monday,
that she saw this bird; grey, small, solitary but contented in its
solitude. Adah stood still on the other side of the road watching this grey bird, singing, singing, hopping from one window ledge to another, happy in its lonely freedom. Adah
was intrigued by the creature. Fancy being moved this early
in the morning by such a small thing as this grey bird,
when less than a year before she had seen wilder birds, all
gaudy in their colours, all wild in their songs. She never took
notice of birds then, in the back yards of Lagos houses. Then
she thought to herself: suppose there was never any winter,
when every living thing seems to disappear from the face
of the earth, the birds would always be around, they would
become an everyday thing, and she wouldn't have noticed
and admired it and listened to its watery song. Was that not
what we need in Africa, to have a long, long winter, when
there would be no sunshine, no birds, no wild flowers and
no warmth? That would make us a nation of introverts,
maybe, and when eventually spring came, then we would
be able to appreciate the songs of birds. What does this
mean? Has Nature been too merciful to us, robbing us of
the ability to wake ourselves up from our tropical slumber
to know that a simple thing like the song of a grey bird on a

wet Monday morning in spring can be inspiring? Was that why the early Europeans who came to Africa thought the black man was lazy because of his over-abundant environment which robbed him of the ability to think for himself? Well, Adah concluded, to cheer herself up, that may be so, but that happened years and years ago, before the birth of her Pa.

She was different. Her children were going to be different. They were all going to be black, they were going to enjoy being black, be proud of being black, a black of a different breed. That's what they were going to be. Had she not now learned to listen to the songs of birds? Was that not one of the natural happenings that inspired her favourite poet, Wordsworth? She might never be a famous poet like Wordsworth, because he was too great, but Adah was going to train herself to admire the songs of the birds however riotous, to appreciate the beauty of flowers however extravagant their scent. She jolted herself to, reminding herself that she was the mother of three babies, and that she was supposed to be rushing for her Monday morning bath.

The woman who cleaned the baths greeted her like an old friend. They knew she was always the first customer on Monday mornings, because Saturdays were usually too busy, and the baths too crowded. She preferred Mondays, when most people had gone to work and the ladies working at the baths would not have to hurry her up. The only snag was that on Monday mornings she seldom got very hot water, because the boiler, or whatever heated the water, had to be turned off over the week-end. It usually took a long time to heat up, but Adah did not mind the lukewarmness of the water, because that was the price she was paying for a long, quiet bath.

Her bath that Monday morning was particularly important, because she was going to the Family Planning Clinic. She had attended the week before and had been loaded with masses of literature. She had read about the jelly, the Pill, the cap and so many other things. She told Francis she was going, but Francis told her not to go because men knew how to control themselves better, the way it was done in the Bible. You hold the child and you don't give it to the woman, you pour it away. Adah considered this. It was not because she had stopped trusting her husband, but her husband could hurt her without meaning to, for wasn't that the way he had been brought up? She knelt and prayed to God to forgive her for making other plans behind her husband's back.

When it was time to take Bubu to the clinic to be weighed, she saw a motherly-looking nurse and told her, 'Please, could I have the Pill? You see, I am not twenty-one yet and if I had another child it would be my fourth, and I originally came here to study and bring up the two babies I brought from home. Can you help me? I need the Pill.'

The woman smiled and tickled Bubu on the cheek. They had a Family Planning Clinic in the evenings on Monday. She would get the literature for Adah to read and she could decide with her husband which would suit them best. Well, how was Adah to tell the woman that Francis said that the best way to control the population was to pour it on the floor? Adah could not bring herself to tell the nurse that. The last nail in the coffin was when the woman brought a form which Adah's husband was supposed to sign to tell them that he was all for it, that he wanted his wife equipped with birth-control gear. There was going to be trouble over that, for Francis would never sign a thing like that, and he would raise hell if he realized that Adah got the literature without his permission. What was Adah going to do? Was it necessary to have a husband brought into an issue like that? Could not the woman be given the opportunity of exercising her own will? Whatever happened, she was not going to have any more children. She did not care which way she achieved this, but she was having no more children. Two boys and a girl were enough for any mother-in-law. If her mother-in-law wanted another one, she could get her son another wife. Adah was not going to have any more. It was not going to be easy for her to forget the experience she had had recently having Bubu. That was a warning. She might not be so lucky next time.

Francis announced that he had read his two chapters scheduled for the day and that he was tired of reading and that he was going down to the Nobles to watch their television. Adah encouraged him to go. She wanted to read the birth-control literature in detail. Adah fished the now rumpled leaflets out from under Bubu's cot where she had hidden them. She read them again and again. Three facts stuck. One was that the Pill is the one you swallow just like aspirin. Secondly, the jelly is the one you allow to melt inside. The cap, which was the third thing, was the one you fitted in. Adah chuckled and was amused at it all. Fancy making a special cap for your other end instead of for your head. Well, those Europeans would stop at nothing. She was not going to choose the cap though, as it would be too messy, messing around with one's insides. No, she would go for the Pill, that was less complicated. The jelly? No, Francis would notice and ask questions.

But how was she to make Francis sign the form? The thought came to her that she could sign it for him. But that would be forgery. She imagined herself at a court and the magistrate sending her to jail for seven years for forging her husband's signature. But at the end of it she would be alive, and once alive, she might be allowed to look after her children. But if she did not forge the signature it might mean another child, another traumatic birth, another mouth to feed; and she was still not getting anywhere with her studies. The price she would have to pay for being an obedient and loyal wife would be too much. She forged the signature. She saved and scraped from the housekeeping money to pay for the first lot of pills. The money had been saved, the form signed, and, to add to her joy, she now had another library job waiting for her at the Chalk Farm Library. She was going to keep this job, no matter what. She was not going to allow herself to get pregnant again. Never.

But first she had to have this Monday bath, in case she had to strip herself to be examined or something. She had told Francis that Babu was such a big baby, gaining weight every day, that the people at the clinic would like his photograph taken that Monday evening. It pained her, having to resort to that very method she had always used when she was little. That horrible tendency to twist the facts. But what else was there for her to do? She prayed to God again and again to forgive her.

She had to take Bubu with her, because if she had not, Francis would have said, 'I thought you told me that the people at the clinic were going to take this photo, because he was such a beautiful baby?' So she took Bubu with her.

At the clinic, she was shown into a waiting-room, where there were other women waiting. Two were undressed with their stockings rolled down round their ankles, just as you are when you are expecting, and the doctor wants to examine you. They reminded Adah of the pre-natal clinics. She was now used to that sort of thing – stripping herself naked to be examined. It did not bother her any more. She asked herself, why should it worry me? I've only got what you've got. Why should I be ashamed of my body? It did not matter any more.

Three screens were set up in the middle of the square room. Women were to undress behind the screen and then sit down and wait to be called one by one into the doctor's room to be equipped with birth-control gear.

Adah saw a young West Indian mother and purposely went and sat down beside her. She wanted to be on home ground because she was frightened and because the young girl was the only woman there holding a baby. Adah could look after her baby when she went in to be equipped, and she could look after Adah's. That would be fair. With such noble thoughts in her mind, she greeted the West Indian girl with a friendly smile. The girl smiled back showing a golden tooth wedged in between her ordinary teeth.

They soon started to talk. She, the West Indian girl, was going to be trained as a nurse, so she needed some form of birth-control during her training. Her husband did not mind. So, months before, she was given the Pill. But, she cried to Adah, see what the Pill had done to her. She pulled up her sleeves and showed Adah a very fine rash. The rash was all over her face and neck. Even her skinny wrists had not been spared. She was covered with the kind of rash that reminded Adah of the rash caused by prickly heat in Africa.

'Do they make you scratch? I mean, do you feel scratchy all the time?'

'Yeah, man. That's the trouble now. I don't mind the appearance. But they itch all the time.'

Adah looked at her face again, and as she did so the girl started to scratch the back of her skirt. She was trying to hide it from the other women, trying to hide the fact that her bottom was itching. God have mercy! thought Adah. Her bottom as well? Then she asked the girl, 'Have you got the itch down there as well?'

The girl nodded. She had it all over her. Adah called to God to have mercy on her again. What was she going to do now? She was not going on the Pill if she was going to end up looking like somebody with chicken-pox, or scratching like this girl as if she was covered with yaws. No, she was not going to have the Pill, and she was not going home empty-handed with no birth-control. She thought about the jelly and knew that it would only work when husband and wife are in agreement, for he would have to wait until it melted before coming on. So the jelly was out of the question for her. She could only go for the cap. That almighty cap which is specially made for one's inside. She had to think quickly. Francis might not know. The business was always done in the dark anyway. But suppose he felt it? Supposing he saw her fixing the cap in their one-room apartment with no bathroom and with the toilet as filthy as a rubbish dump? She could not fix the cap in the toilet, for what would happen if the cap fell? It would have collected enough germs to send her to her Maker in no time with cancer of the bottom. Adah was sure you could get cancer easily from under there. What was she going to do now? If only Francis would be reasonable. Whatever happened, she was going to risk it. A cap was better than nothing.

It came to her turn to go and see the doctor and the midwife who fixed you up with your own special size of cap. It was a messy job. They kept trying this and that and kept scolding Adah to relax otherwise she would go home with the wrong cap that would not fit her properly and *that* would mean another child. The fear of what Francis would say and what he would write to his mother and her relations loomed, full of doom, in her subconscious. Only she could feel it. The other two females, who were now tut-tutting at her and growing impatient and telling her to relax her legs, could not see the same picture that Adah was seeing. It was the picture of her mother-in-law when she heard that Adah went behind her husband's back to equip herself with something that would allow her to sleep around and not have any more children. She was sure they would interpret it that way, knowing the psychology of her people. The shame of it would kill her. Her children's name would be smeared as well. God, don't let Francis find out. In desperation, the two women, the doctor and the midwife gave her a size of cap that they thought should fit. If it did not fit, it was not their fault, because Adah did not help them at all because she was feeling so guilty of what she was doing. First she had forged her husband's signature, now she had got a cap which she was sure was going to cause a row if he found out. But suppose he did not find out and suppose it worked? That would mean no children and she would keep her new job and finish her course in librarianship. With that happy thought, she put the new equipment in Bubu's pram and went home.

But when she got home, she was faced with another problem. How was she to know what was going to happen on a particular night? Must she then wear the cap every night? That was the safest thing, but the cap was not very comfortable and Adah knew that it wobbled and she had to walk funnily to keep it in. And of course Francis would know. Oh, God, if only they had an extra room, then Francis would not have to see and watch and to make irritating remarks about her every move!

She ran down to their back yard toilet that had no electric light and fitted herself with her new cap. She could hear Titi and Vicky having their usual fight, and soon Francis would start calling for her to come and quieten her children. She fitted the cap in a hurry, almost going sick at the thought of it all. At that moment she felt really sorry for doctors and nurses. The amount of messing they have to do with people's insides! She dashed up, for Francis was already calling her and asking her what the hell it was she was doing down there in the toilet. Was she having another baby down there? Adah looked blank and said nothing. The fact that she was quiet made Francis suspicious. He then asked her what the matter was. Adah said that nothing was the matter.

He looked at her again and asked, 'Have you got a boil or something?'

Adah turned round from where she was tucking the kids into bed and asked, 'What boil?'

And Francis, still looking intensely at her, replied: 'Boil in the leg. You walk funny.'

Adah smiled, a wobbly, uncertain sort of smile, for her heart was beating so fast and so loudly, the noice was like a Nigerian housewife pounding yams in her *Odo*. Her heart was going 'gbim, gbim, gbim,' just like that. She was surprised and shocked to realize that Francis could not hear the guilty beating of that heart of hers. She thought everybody could hear it because it was so loud to her that it hurt in her chest, making it difficult to breathe. But she managed a smile, that sort of lying smile. And it worked wonders.

Then she said, just to press home another point, 'You were calling me so loudly when I was down there in the back yard, that I ran up the stairs, and I bumped my toe on one of them, and it hurts a bit.'

Francis arched his brows but said nothing.

Soon it was midnight, and the row which Adah had dreaded flared up. Francis got the whole truth out of her. So, she a married woman, married in the name of God and again married in the name of Oboshi, the goddess of Ibuza, came to London and became clever enough within a year to go behind his back and equip herself with a cap which he, Francis, was sure had been invented for harlots and single women. Did Adah not know the gravity of what she had done? It meant she could take other men behind his back, because how was he to know that she was not going to do just that if she could go and get the gear behind his back? Francis called all the other tenants to come and see and hear about this great issue – how the innocent Adah who came to London only a year previously had become so clever. Adah was happy when Pa Noble came, because at least it made Francis stop hitting her. She was dizzy with pain and her head throbbed. Her mouth was bleeding. And once or twice during the proceedings she felt tempted to run out and call the police. But she thought better of it. Where would she go after that? She had no friends and she had no relations in London.

Francis made it clear that he was writing to his mother and father. Adah was not surprised at this. But she was frightened, for despite everything she still respected her mother-in-law. But her son Francis was severing the ties of friendship that existed between Adah and his family. She knew that, after that, things were not going to be the same any more. She cried then. She was lonely again, just as she was when Pa died and Ma married again and she had to live in a relative's house.

Her marriage with Francis? It was finished as soon as Francis called in the Nobles and the other tenants. She told herself that she could not live with such a man. Now everybody knew she was being knocked about, only a few weeks after she had come out of hospital. Everybody now knew that the man she was working for and supporting was not only a fool, but that he was too much of a fool to know that he was acting foolishly. Pa Noble reminded Francis of Adah's health and God bless the old man, he sent all the inquisitive tenants away. There was nothing bad in Adah getting birth-control gear, Pa Noble said, but she should have told her husband.

What was the point of Adah telling them that she had told her husband and he had said you could control children by pouring them on the floor? But it did not matter. She was almost twenty-one. And, among her people, a girl of twenty-one was no longer a girl, but a woman who could make decisions. Let Francis write to her people and his people. If she liked, she would read their letters, if she did not she could throw them into the fire. The only person that mattered was her brother. She would write and tell him the truth. Boy had never liked Francis anyway. He knew even before Adah found out that Francis looked like those men who could live off women because of his good looks. Adah had just left school and was full of the religious idea that you could change anybody by your own personal example and by prayers. She was wrong and Boy her brother was right.

A few weeks later, Francis had his examination result, and

it was another failure. Of course the fault was Adah's, especially as she managed to scrape through a part of her library examination. To explain his failures Francis wrote to his parents about the cap. But by the time their reply came, Adah was being eaten up by another problem. She was pregnant again.

12 The Collapse

Yes, Adah was pregnant again. This time she did not cry, she did not wring her hands, but behaved philosophically. If this pattern was going to be her lot in life she would do all she could to change it, but what was she going to do if all her efforts failed?

She went to her Indian doctor. She told him her whole story and that she wanted the pregnancy terminated. The Indian doctor was not a young man at all, but he had a certain way of saying things and was so small that one could easily take him for a young man. He had made good in London and had two sons who were both up at Cambridge; he had married a woman doctor he met when he was a student himself. He was very popular among the blacks living in that part of Kentish Town at the time. Adah guessed that if she appealed to him, being Indian and once a student in London, he would understand her predicament.

He understood, shook his head, sympathized and said, 'You should have come to us for the cap. The ones at the clinic are cheap ones and they go loose quickly. You should have told me about it.'

That was very nice. That was what Adah ought to have done if she had known. But how was she supposed to know? Smell it out like a witch doctor? Had he and his wife not put a notice in the waiting-room about the danger of smoking? Could they not have had a similar notice to say that birth-control was available for the asking? It was too late now. She was pregnant, she knew it, but the doctor told her that it was too early for confirmation. He would give her some white pills. Adah was to take them and they would work.

Adah wondered what those pills were meant to do for her. But in her state of apathetic resignation, she did not ask questions. The pills were going to terminate the pregnancy.

If the pregnancy was going to be terminated, what was the point of telling Francis? How did she know he would not misunderstand? Even if he did understand, how could she be sure he was not going to repeat it to the Nobles, to his parents and to everybody? Could she tell Francis and say, 'Look, I am telling you this under the seal of the confessional. You must not repeat it.' That would be impossible.

She now saw this situation as a challenge, a new challenge. When she was little and alone, the challenge had been that of educating herself, existing through it all, alone, all by herself. She had hoped that in marriage she could get herself involved in her man's life and he would share the same involvement in hers. She had gambled with marriage, just like most people, but she had gambled unluckily and had lost. Now she was alone again with this new challenge that included her children as well. She was going to live, to survive, to exist through it all. Some day, help would come from somewhere. She had been groping for that help as if she were in the dark. Some day her fingers would touch something solid that would help her pull herself out. She was becoming aware of that Presence again – the Presence that had directed her through childhood. She went nearer to It in her prayers. She never knelt down to pray in the orthodox way. But she talked to Him while stirring peppery African soup on her cooker; she talked to Him when she woke up in the morning; she talked to Him all the time, and Adah felt that He was always there.

There was no time to go to church and pray. Not in England. It took her years to erase the image of the Nigerian church which usually had a festive air. In England, especially in London, 'church' was a big grey building with stained-glass windows, high ornamental ceilings, very cold, full of rows and rows of empty chairs, with the voice of the vicar droning from the distant pulpit, crying like the voice of John the Baptist lost in the wilderness. In London, churches were cheerless.

She could not go to any of them because it made her cry to see such beautiful places of worship empty when, in Nigeria, you could hardly get a seat if you came late. You had to stand outside and follow the service through a microphone. But you were happy through it all, you were encouraged to bellow out the songs – that bellowing took away some of your sorrows. Because most of the hymns seem to be written by psychologists. One was always sure of singing or hearing something that would come near to the problem you had in mind before coming to church. In England you were robbed of such comfort.

London, having thus killed Adah's congregational God, created instead a personal God who loomed large and really alive. She did not have to go to church to see this One. He was always there, when she was shelving books in the libary, when she was tucking her babies up to sleep, when she was doing anything. She grew nearer to Him, to the people with whom she worked, but away from Francis. The gulf between them which had grown with her stay in hospital had been made deeper by the cap incident, and now this new child would make it greater still. But she was not going to tell Francis and she did not feel guilty about it. Francis would not be of any help.

She concentrated on working and enjoying her new job. It was at the Chalk Farm Library that she met Peggy, the Irish girl with a funny hair style, who was heartbroken because her Italian summer-holiday boy-friend did not fulfil his promises. Peggy had gone on holiday the summer before, just to enjoy the Italian sun and the Roman scenery. She got involved with this handsome Italian youth, surprisingly tall for an Italian, but Peggy said he was Italian. It was love at first sight, and many promises were made. Peggy was a library assistant and the young man was reading Engineering in a university, the name of which Adah had forgotten. The young man seemed to have forgotten the promises he had made Peggy, and she was threatening to go to the address he gave her to find him and give him a piece of her mind. The talk was always of this young man and what Peggy was going to do to him, and how she was going to get her own back. Peggy never really told Adah what it was she had given him that pained her so much. But she let Adah know that she gave so much that she would regret it all her life. She was twenty-three, not very beautiful but small and fun to be with.

Then there was the big boss, Mr Barking. He was thin and bad-tempered, but without a touch of malice. His daughter had married a worthless fellow and he was determined to squash that marriage if it cost him his life. That daughter was ill because of the mental cruelty being inflicted on her by this no-good husband. Mr Barking never talked about his wife; he had got so used to her being there, in his home, that she was never discussed. That wife of his made good chicken sandwiches. Adah had seen Mr Barking munching and munching away at lots of chicken sandwiches in the staff room, and sometimes they made her feel like having one.

Bill was a big handsome Canadian; Adah did not know why he had come to England in the first place, because he looked down on anything English. He used the word 'Britisher' for the English, just like the Americans do. Even his Christmas cake was flown out from Canada. His mother sent him clothes, food, everything. He would not study for the British Library Association Examinations because he did not trust the British system of education. He had married the children's librarian the year before. Her name was Eileen and she was tall and beautiful, a more perfect match you could never imagine. But Bill knew a little about everything. He liked black writers. Adah did not know any black writers apart from a few Nigerian ones, like Chinua Achebe and Flora Nwapa, and she did not know that there were any other black writers. Bill tut-tutted at her and told her what a shame it was that an intelligent black girl like her should know so little about her own black people. Adah thought about it and realized that Bill was right. He was an intelligen⸱ man, that Canadian, and Adah liked him a lot. During the staff break he would talk and expand about authors and their new books. He would then request it and the Camden Borough would buy it, and he would read it first; then he would pass it on to Adah and she would pass it to Peggy. Peggy would pass it to any other members of the staff who were in the mood to read books. It was through Bill that Adah knew of James Baldwin. She came to believe, through reading Baldwin, that black was beautiful. She asked Bill about it and he said, did she not know that black was beautiful.

Bill was the first real friend she had had outside her family. She had a tendency to trust men more because her Pa never let her down. She had already cultivated a taste for wide reading, and Bill, whose wife was expecting a second child within two years of their marriage, was always in the mood for literary talk. Adah was fascinated. She even started reading Marx and was often quoting to herself that if the worst came to the very worst she would leave Francis with her children since she had nothing to lose but her chains.

She got into the light-hearted atmosphere in which the library staff did their work. There was another girl, a half-caste West Indian, one of the people who found it difficult to claim to be black. She liked Adah because Adah was at that stage forcing everybody to like her. The people at that library made her forget her troubles. Everybody seemed to have troubles then. Bill's wife was having another baby and their flat was very small. He was toying with the idea of going back to his old job, for he had been a radio news-caster in Canada. Why did he come here in the first place? Adah had wondered. He gave the hint, very tentatively, that he was running away from his mother who seemed to have organized a girl she wanted him to marry. He came to England to escape, but then he had met Eileen. Poor man, he was too handsome to be left alone. He was a six footer. Peggy's problem was money to take her to Italy, where she hoped to get a working holiday in order to look for the young Italian who had lied to her. Mr Barking seldom joined in their light-hearted talk, but they all knew he was thinking of his daughter. Fay did not like to associate herself with the black people because she was too white, a mulatto. So, to press home this point, when she qualified as a librarian, she got engaged to this English man who was away in Cambridge reading Law. Adah never saw this man, but she saw Fay's car which was so smashed that it was going to cost Fay a fortune to repair. Fay said her boy-friend had smashed it. Adah was sorry for her, particularly as, although she was very beautiful in a film-star type of way with smooth, glossy skin, a perfect figure and thick beautiful hair, she was at least thirty. And thirty seemed an enormous age to Adah at the time. A woman of thirty and not married was to her an outrage then.

When everybody started talking about their problems, Adah would start laughing.

Peggy would say, 'What the bloody hell are you laughing for?'

Then Bill would reply for her: 'She has no problems. She's happily married to a brilliant husband who is reading to be a Cost and Works accountant, and she is already going through all her library examinations . . .'

Adah would not contradict him. Was the world not too full of sadness? What was the point of telling them all her woes? Yes, they all believed she had no problems because she wanted them all to believe that.

Three months passed speedily in this way and she knew that the pills the doctor had given her had not worked. She told herself not to panic. Women had been caught in worse situations before. Francis would only laugh and say: 'I thought you were being clever, getting the cap behind my back.' She had been through the worst. Even his beatings and slappings did not move her any more. She did not know where she got her courage from, but she was beginning to hit him back, even biting him when need be. If that was the language he wanted, well, she would use it. Was she not the greatest biter in her school? Francis threatened to break all her teeth for her, and grew his nails as long as those of a tiger, so whenever Adah opened her mouth to bite, Francis would dig his tiger nails into her flesh, almost choking her. Then the thought struck her that she could be killed and the world would think it was an accident. Just a husband and wife fighting. She still hit back occasionally when she knew she was near the door or out of danger, but she gave in to his demands for the sake of peace. They were like the demands of a wicked child who enjoys torturing a live animal given to him as a pet.

Adah wanted to know the truth from the doctor before she started looking for a room for herself and her children. Mr Noble was fed up with their fights and had asked them to move. To cap it all, the women in the house wrote Adah an open petition begging her to control her husband, because he was chasing them all. The letter was posted unsealed, and sent to the wrong branch of the library. So other library assistants could read it if they liked. Adah was not worried, she was going anyway.

She waited patiently for her turn at the surgery, then went in. The doctor greeted her and asked her how she was and she said, 'The child is sitting there pretty. It did not come out as you made me believe it was going to.' Her voice was low and panicky for the first time.

The look the doctor gave her was terrible. It seemed to chill her blood. His dark Indian skin seemed to have gone a shade darker. He was making an effort to speak but the anger inside him was choking him so that he gobbled feebly just like a kettle on the boil . . . then just like the kettle he spluttered: 'I did not give you the pills to abort the child.'

Adah recoiled like a frightened snake, but again, like a snake, she was gathering all her inner energy ready to attack this frightened little man. What did he mean? Adah asked with a voice that had a tinge of brutal sharpness in it. She felt like digging her teeth into those eyes that were popping out like a dead fish's.

'All right, so I am having the baby. But I'll tell you this, the pills you gave me were abortive and you know it and I know it, because I carry the child and know what happened the first few weeks you gave them to me. If my child is imperfect in any way, you are responsible. You know that.'

She walked out of the surgery, not to her own home, but to a park near Gospel Oak village and then sat down, thinking. She had suspected something like this would happen, but to have it confirmed this way made her feel a traitor. She cried for herself, she cried for her children, and she cried for the unborn child. Suppose the child was born imperfect, just like those unfortunate Thalidomide babies, what was she going to do then? Her thoughts went to her brother, Boy, who had sent her all his savings, asking her to leave Francis and his children and come back to Nigeria where her work at the Consulate would be waiting for her. Boy, poor Boy, he was very much annoyed over this cap issue which Francis had written to his parents about. The child would give them another song to sing. They would ask why, if she was on birth-control, which she went and got herself, did she then become pregnant? They would say the child was not her husband's, that it'd probably be a white child. You know, like the people who fitted the cap. And then everybody would laugh. Her own people would cover their faces in shame. She found herself being grateful that her parents were dead. This would have killed them. She had raised everybody's hopes when she was at the Methodist Girls' High School, she had raised their hopes higher when she got strings of 'A' levels by taking correspondence courses, and the hopes were being realized when she was in a good job at the American Consulate. If only she had stopped then. She could have passed the rest of her examinations by correspondence. After all, was Ibadan University not a branch of the great *London* University she was so mad about?

But would her children have been in this kind of nursery school where they were then? She got confused. Had it all been worth it?

Then a hand touched her shoulder. The hand was a black man's. Adah jumped. Sitting there, thinking and shedding silent tears, she had not heard the man cross the park. He was an African, a Nigerian. And when he spoke, Adah knew he was an Ibo.

'You've had a fight with your husband?'

Adah did not answer. The man went on:

'My name is Okpara, and I know you are Ibo because of the marks on your face. I don't want to hear anything. Let's go and beg his forgiveness. He would let you in.' Typical Ibo psychology; men never do wrong, only the women; they have to beg for forgiveness, because they are bought, paid for and must remain like that, silent obedient slaves.

Adah showed him the way to her house. Had not the magic pass word 'Ibo' been uttered? The man talked all the way about this and that. They had been here some time and were getting ready to go home in about four months. His wife was a secretary and he worked in the Civil Service here. He had now finished his studies. But, he told Adah, they still quarrelled, though he would never beat his wife. He had out-grown that, but they still quarrelled. These quarrels did not mean the end of marriage. He reminded Adah of an old Ibo saying.

'Don't you remember, or have you forgotten, the saying of our people, that a husband and his wife always build their home for many things but particularly for quarrels? A home is where you quarrel in.' Adah nodded, she did remember.

She should have asked Mr Okpara whether the old people lived in one room, whether the men gave babies to their wives in such quick succession. Had not her Ma told her that during her time they used to nurse and breast-feed a child for at least three years? At least those men, the men of the time Mr Okpara was talking about, had other amusements. They had their tribal dances, they had their age-group meetings from which they arrived too drunk with palm-wine to have the energy to ask for their wives. Superstition played a big role in the lives of those people; if you slept with your wife when she was nursing a child, the child would die, so husbands abstained from their nursing wives for a period of three years. Many men were polygamous for this reason. They would build a separate hut for the nursing wife, pension her off for that long period and take in a childless one. These people could afford to build a house in which to quarrel.

But not in London, where her Francis sat all week in the same room by the same kitchen table turning the pages of this book and that book, getting up only to eat or go down to the Nobles to watch their television. Francis could never have a mind as healthy as those men. Again it struck her that their plan had failed, and that it had been all her fault. She should not have agreed to work all the time. She should have encouraged Francis to work, just like this man's wife, whom she had not seen, had encouraged her husband to work. Francis would have met other men, like this one, and he would have copied them. It was not too late, she consoled herself. That was what she was going to try to do. It might even still save the marriage. After all had not Mr Okpara studied privately in the evenings and still gained a certificate instead of going to watch the television from six o'clock to closedown?

To Mr Okpara she said nothing because she still maintained to herself that failure to make her marriage work
was her own affair. She did not mind listening to the story
of a successful one, and maybe getting some tips on how
to make hers work, but she was not letting this stranger
know. Why did she allow Mr Okpara to come home with her?
Adah herself did not know the answer. She did not tell the
man anything, even though her mind was crying for someone to listen to her, to understand her. Yet she felt that by
talking to this stranger, although he was kind and an Ibo
like herself, she would be betraying her husband, her family,
her children. You don't tell people your troubles when you
are still in the midst of them, otherwise it makes them bigger,
more insoluble. You tell people when it's all over, then
others can learn from your mistakes, and then you can afford
to laugh over it. Because by then they have stopped hurting,
you have passed them all, have graduated from them.

They got into their room. The scene that met their eyes
was comical, and that was an understatement. Vicky was
sitting on the settee, waving his wet nappy in the air like a
flag. Titi was perched on the bed, looking thoughtfully at
Vicky and their father. Bubu was lying flat on his back in the
cot, listening to the songs Francis was singing to his children
from the Jehovah's Witnesses handbook, looking as untidy
as ever. His unshaved face became more noticeable now that
Mr Okpara was in the room. The latter was darker than
Francis; he was not tall, about five foot eight, the same height
as Francis, but he was immaculate. His white shirt was
dazzling, and the fact that he was very black pronounced the
whiteness still further. He was wearing a black three-piece
suit, and his black shoes shone. His black briefcase added to
his dignity somehow and the black rolled umbrella he was
carrying completed the image – a black bank clerk in Britain
coming home from the city.

As for Francis, to Adah he did not look like the image of
anything. He was just himself, just Francis Obi, and Adah
saw then that if she was going to model him on the image
of this Mr Okpara, she was going to have a big fight ahead
of her. Francis was Francis, not ashamed of being Francis,
and was not going to change, even if Adah brought two

hundred successful Ibo students to show him. He was proud to be what he was and Adah had better start getting used to him that way or move out.

Francis swore to Mr Okpara that he did not touch Adah. 'She simply went out. I did not know where, but I knew she would come back because she can't bear to leave her children for long. I did not beat her. Did she say that?'

Okpara was not daunted. They were not happy. Adah was not happy and this country was a dangerous place to be unhappy in, because you have nobody to pour out your troubles to, so that was why most lonely African students usually had emotional breakdowns because they had no one to share their troubles with. Did Francis want *his* wife to have such a breakdown? Okpara asked. Would that not be a drain on his purse?

This startled Francis and Adah. She did not know that people still lived like that, the husband paying for the doctor's bills. Even in Nigeria, whenever it was necessary for a private doctor to be called, she had always paid. She could not remember Francis ever paying for anything like that. Okpara was out of touch with the problem at hand, and Francis, now confused with anger, shame and disappointment, resented this intrusion into his family life. Adah hurried to make coffee.

She did not know that Francis had come to such a situation that he had told himself subconsciously that he would never pass his examinations. He had as it were told himself that his ever becoming a Cost and Works accountant in this world was a dream. She did not know that for this reason he would do everything to make Adah a failure like himself. He could not help it, it was human nature. He was not a bitter man.

He lashed his tongue at Okpara, told him to go back home and mind his own business. It was then that Adah realized that Okpara was English only on the surface. An English person would have felt insulted and would leave. But not Okpara. He was Ibo, and this was an Ibo family in trouble, and he was not going to leave until he had made them promise to pay a visit, so that they would see how the Okparas lived. He asked Adah if she had relations in London. Could they not intervene for her?

Adah thought this over. She had no close relatives in London, and the few distant ones would simply laugh. They would say: 'We thought she was the educated lady who knew all the answers. Did we not warn her against marrying that man? Did she not make her own bed? Well, let her sleep in it!' So Adah shook her head and said she had nobody.

After coffee, Okpara talked and advised Francis to be a man. Staying at home, and singing to his children from the hymn book of the Jehovah's Witnesses would not feed and clothe his family, to say nothing of his old parents at home. So he must get a job and study in the evenings. After all, the subjects were not completely new to him any more. Otherwise he would lose his manhood, and these children that he was singing to would soon realize that it was their mother that bought them clothes and food.

Francis stared at him as he said this, because it was a great humiliation to an African not to be respected by his own children. Okpara noticed that he had touched a soft spot for he then banged at the kitchen table, just to emphasize his point. He went on and said did Francis not know that the children born in this country get clever right from their mother's stomach? They know and they can remember what goes on around them. So if Francis wanted to hold the respect of his two sons, he'd better know what he was doing. Okpara did not mention Titi, she was only a girl, a second-class human being; it did not matter whether she respected her father or not. She was going to grow into an ordinary woman not a complete human like a man.

In the weeks and months that followed Okpara and his pretty little wife did their best but Francis would always be Francis. He had been used to being worked for, by a woman whom he knew belonged to him by right. Adah could not escape because of the children or so Francis thought.

When she told him she was expecting another child, the laughter that greeted this announcement was like a mad monkey's in the zoo. It was so animal-like, so inhuman, so mirthless, and yet so brutal. Adah was sure she was five months gone before she told him. She had first got over the pain in her own mind, but was still anxious about the perfection of the baby. She worried about that sometimes, but one thing she had learned from Bubu's confinement was that she was not going to that hospital as a poor nigger woman. Her baby was going to arrive in style. She knitted and sewed, and this time her maternity grant was not going to Francis. She was buying a brand-new pram, a new shawl and a new outfit for herself for when she came out of the hospital. She met a West Indian girl who had had a baby girl by a Nigerian; but the man had not married her because, according to him, the child was not his. It was this girl who showed Adah that you could live on what was called the Assistance until your children grew up and you could get a job. Adah had heard of this Assistance before, in Nigeria; she learnt about it in her Social History lessons. She did not know that she could still claim it. If only she had known, she would have left Francis earlier. But she did not know.

She addressed twenty greeting cards to herself, gave three pounds to Irene, the girl, and told her to post three cards a day after the baby was born. Two big bunches of flowers were to be sent to her, one on her arrival, with Francis's name attached to it with sentimental words. The other was to arrive at the hospital after her safe delivery. But if she did not survive the birth, Irene was to put Adah's children's names on it and make it into a wreath. Irene got sentimental and started to cry; Adah told her not to, because we all have to die some time. She was sure that if she was going to be operated upon like before, she did not have much chance. But the Indian doctor, now sorry for what he had done, had become Adah's strongest ally. The chances of her not being operated upon were fifty-fifty. Adah knew that if there was one single chance of her not being cut up, she was going to take that one chance. Her body had a way of rejecting anything foreign, she had known that too. So instead of handing over her pay packet to Francis to dole out the two pounds for housekeeping to her she would buy everything the doctors and the midwives told her to eat. Francis raised many rows, but Adah had a more important thing to worry about – her unborn child. It was so small she could hardly feel it. Her figure did not get big like it did when she was having the others. But she kept strictly to the diet prescribed.

It was then that she was introduced to the modern way of relaxation birth. Adah attended all the classes. It all seemed so easy that she regretted the unnecessary pain she had experienced with the other children. She did not lie about the date of her confinement and she was determined to have her four weeks' rest before going into hospital.

The money was not enough to go round and she told Francis, 'From now on, fend for yourself. I know the children are mine, because they need to be fed. You must go out and work. If not, I shall only cater for my children.'

Francis told her that she could not do it. Adah said nothing, but carried out her plans. He must go out to work. She cared about his studies and all that, but the children were growing both in size and in number. They came first. They had a right to happiness as well, not just Francis. He told her to write down the statement that she would not feed him any more. Adah wrote it without any hesitation. If the world was going to blame her for not feeding her able-bodied husband, let it go ahead. She did not care any more. She had three children to think about and soon there would be four.

They were sorry at the Chalk Farm Library that she was going. She was sorry too, but there, in that library, she discovered a hidden talent which she did not know she had before – the uninhibited ability to make friends easily. People had a way of trusting her easily because she was always trying to laugh however bad the situation. She learned to avoid gloomy people; they made her unhappy. So, since she could not avoid seeing Francis and his sad face, she shut him off from her mind's eye. She saw him but her mind did not register him any more. She heard him say that he had reported her to a Ministry or Board or something because she had signed that she would not feed him any more. Adah waited for the Law to come for her, but the Law did not.

He came with her to the hospital in the ambulance, though. On the second morning of her stay, her big bunch of flowers arrived. Her table was gay with cards even before Dada

176

arrived. She came that night, small, but painless, and perfect. Adah was sure that the child arrived in the world smiling and laughing. She was so small, less than five pounds in weight, but beautiful, just like a black doll – and a girl. Adah was thankful for this child, so perfect and beautiful that she nicknamed her 'Sunshine'.

She came home by herself in a taxi, and did it in style. She made everybody believe that she had wanted it so, to surprise her husband. She did not tell them that Francis had refused to come for her. They would start to pity her, and she could do without that. She tipped the nurses generously and they all laughed and thanked her. When she got home, she wrote a very nice letter to them all thanking them and she could hear them in her mind's ear saying what a nice happy African woman she was. She had no troubles in the world. Because of this attitude her problems became insignificant. They were all part of her life.

Hunger drove Francis to work as a clerical officer in the Post Office. Adah's hopes rose. This might save the marriage after all. But she was disappointed. Francis would pay the rent and still gave her only two pounds for the six of them and nothing more. Adah did not know how much he was earning or when he was paid. She warned him, though, that she was going into the Civil Service herself, and that she was going to do the same thing. She would not pay the rent, because it was a man's job to do that, she would not contribute to the food budget, because was she not his wife? She would only be responsible for her children, their clothes, the nursery fees and anything else the children needed. But Francis would not know how much she earned or on what date, because he had started it. He told her that she could not do that because she was his wife. He could refuse to allow her to go out to work. Then Adah retorted saying:

'This is England, not Nigeria. I don't need your signature to secure a job for me.'

But Adah hoped and prayed that this new sense of awareness and of pride in himself would continue. He bought himself a suit and shirts, he bought a small transistor radio, which Adah and the children were not allowed to touch and which he carried with him wherever he went, to work and even to the toilet. Adah laughed inside herself, and said how like a small boy Francis could be. She paid for her own food and the children's from the little savings she had collected from the superannuation pay. For the roof over their heads, she paid by being a wife to Francis at night, and by washing his endless shirts.

Her baby grew stronger, and she paid off her conscience by breast-feeding her. She was not going to bottle-feed this one. She had read somewhere that breast-fed babies were more intelligent, and grew stronger, than those fed from the bottle. She learned, too, that there was less likelihood of the mother becoming pregnant again if she did that. So she breast-fed her child.

Things seemed to be working out well, but Adah's money was running short, and the children needed new clothes. She worked out a timetable, and found that she could manage to have three hours of quiet each afternoon. Then her old dream came popping up. Why not attempt writing? She had always wanted to write. Why not? She ran to Foyle's and bought herself a *Teach Yourself to Write* and sat down throughout all those months when she was nursing Dada and wrote the manuscript of a book she was going to call *The Bride Price*.

13 The Ditch Pull

That year's summer was glorious. Dada was born in May and since Adah had brought her home from the hospital the sun had never stopped shining. The English people say that, in England, long warm summers always follow cold and horrible winters, which may or may not be so, but for that year the saying was correct.

Adah enjoyed it all the more, because for the first time in her life she was a real housewife. It only lasted five months, but how she wished that her life pattern could have continued that way. She did not rush back to work after having Dada because she had told her husband that with four children all under five, she could not bear to leave them with another woman. Titi's name had been put down for a nursery school attached to Carlton School, just off Queen's Crescent. All Adah had to do every day was to take Titi to school, do her shopping at the Crescent, take the babies to the park for an hour or two, come home, give them their lunch, tuck them up to rest, and write her *The Bride Price*.

If Francis had been an Englishman, or if Francis had not been Francis but somebody else, it would have worked and Adah would have willingly packed up her studies just to be a housewife. She had been reading a great number of women's magazines, and was surprised to read of mothers saying that they were bored just being housewives. She was not that type of woman. There were so many things she planned to do, and she did them. She knitted endless jumpers and cardigans for everybody, including thick big ones for Francis. It was a way of telling him that that was all she asked of life. Just to be a mother and a wife.

But Francis was from another culture. There was a conflict going on in his head. What was the point of marrying an educated woman? Why had his parents been asked to pay a big price if all she was going to do was to come to England and start modelling her life on that of English women, not wanting to work, just sitting there doing nothing but washing the babies' nappies? To him he was being cheated. He had to work, study in the evenings and on Saturdays whilst Adah sat there doing nothing. He started to stay away from work on any pretext. When it rained heavily, Francis was sure he would catch cold. He would not leave home until it was about ten minutes to nine, and he was supposed to be at work by nine. Adah pointed out to him over and over again that it would take him at least thirty minutes to get to his place of work. But Francis did not listen to her. The first glamour of his new power, the power gained by the knowledge that, for the first time in their married life, he was bringing in the money, had died. He saw that Adah was not moved by this new power because the money he gave her for housekeeping was just enough to buy his own food. Adah did not mind. When she had spent all her super-annuation she was going to start taking in clothes to sew for the clothing factory off the Crescent. The man who owned the factory was pleased with the specimen she had shown him and promised to give her a part-time job when she was ready. Adah liked this because it meant she could work at home and look after the children, but the best reason was that Francis would be away from home, rubbing shoulders with other men. Just fancy her, being married at last in the real sense, just like any other woman.

It was in that happy mood that she went to the small branch of Woolworth's off the Crescent and bought four school exercise books, and started to scribble down *The Bride Price*. The more she wrote, the more she knew she could write and the more she enjoyed writing. She was feeling this urge: *Write; go on and do it, you can write.* When she finished it and read it all through, she knew she had no message with a capital 'M' to tell the world, because it was full of scenes with sickly adolescent love sentiments. A recent film which she had seen not long ago awoke the same feeling in her as that first literary attempt of hers did. The story was over-romanticized. Adah had put everything that was lacking in her marriage into it. During the time

180

she was writing it, she was oblivious of everything except her children. Writing, to her, was like listening to good sentimental music. It mattered little to her whether it was published or not, all that mattered was that she had written a book.

In her happiness she forgot that Francis came from another culture, that he was not one of those men who would adapt to new demands with ease, that his ideas about women were still the same. To him, a woman was a second-class human, to be slept with at any time, even during the day, and, if she refused, to have sense beaten into her until she gave in; to be ordered out of bed after he had done with her; to make sure she washed his clothes and got his meals ready at the right time. There was no need to have an intelligent conversation with his wife because, you see, she might start getting ideas. Adah knew she was a thorn in his flesh. She understood what he was going through because he was suffering so. But although she was sorry for him, although she understood all that was happening to him, she was not going to be that kind of a wife. Francis could beat her to death but she was not going to stoop to that level. But all the time she kept hoping that his long stay in England would change him. Did they not come to England for further studies? Surely he would change somehow. Adah knew that she was changing herself. Many things that had mattered and had worried her before had become less important. For instance, it did not matter to her any more whether she became a librarian or a seamstress. What mattered was that she should not be bothered with unhappiness, because she wanted to radiate happiness to all those around her. And when she was happy, she noticed that her children were happy too. But when they saw their father slapping her or telling her off, they clung to her, afraid, their eyes roaming this way and that in childish terror.

She was going to show *The Bride Price* to Francis, to show him that she could write and that she had not been wasting her time as he thought. But first she must take the manuscript to her friends at the Chalk Farm Library.

Bill read it and so did Peggy and the others. She thought they would laugh and tell her that it was a good first attempt. But Bill took it quite seriously. She should show it to somebody in publishing! This scared Adah. She did not know anybody in publishing, she did not know whether she could type the whole lot. It was so enormous, that manuscript. The words, simple, not sophisticated at all, kept pouring from her mind. She had written it, as if it were someone talking, talking fast, who would never stop. Now Bill said it was good, she should get it typed out, and he was going to show it to somebody. It was imperative now that Adah should tell her Francis.

She renewed her books, tucked them neatly in between Bubu and Dada in the pram, mopped Vicky's running nose, and they all marched to Carlton School to collect Titi from the nursery. But Adah was deep in thought as they crossed Haverstock Hill into Prince of Wales Road, pushing the pram with Vicky trotting by her side, the sun shining in the sky, the day hot and merry like any day in Africa. People were passing her this way and that, all in colourful sleeveless summer dresses, one or two old dears sitting on the benches by the side of the Crescent in front of the pub smiling, showing their stiff dentures, their crooked hat pulled down to shade their tired heads from the unusual sun. She walked into the Crescent where the smell of ripe tomatoes mingled with the odour from the butcher's. But she saw none of this, her mind was turning over so fast. Could Peggy and Bill be right? Could she be a writer, a real one? Did she feel totally fulfilled when she had completed the manuscript, just as if it was another baby she had had? 'I felt so fulfilled when I finished it, just as if I had just made another baby,' she had told Bill, and he had replied: 'But that is how writers feel. Their work is their brainchild. This is your brainchild; you are the only one in this whole world who could have produced that particular work, no one else could. If they tried it would just be an imitation. Books tell a great deal about the writers. It is like your own particular child.'

The phrase kept coming and going through Adah's mind. *Brainchild, brainchild.* Francis must see it. They might never publish it, she knew, but she was going to use that as a stepping stone. She had always dreamed of becoming a writer, but she had told herself that writers knew so much that before she made her first attempt at collecting her knowledge

182

into a book she would be at least forty. But now she had done *The Bride Price*, as a joke at first, but realizing that she was serious as she scribbled along. Now a few of her friends had read it and they said that it was good.

She would study harder, then, to be a writer. But where would she start? There was such a lot, and such a diverse lot, one had to know to be a writer. She could not write in any African language, so it must be English although English was not her mother tongue. Yes, it was the English language she was going to use. But she could not write those big long twisting words. Well, she might not be able to do those long difficult words, but she was going to do her own phrases her own way. Adah's phrases, that's what they were going to be. But first she would need guidance. The simplest books she could think of were the Bible and the complete works of Shakespeare. Her Pa had taught her how to read by the Bible, St Matthew in the Bible, that part which said that there were fourteen generations after David before the birth of Christ. She ended up knowing most of the words of that part of the Bible by heart. As for Shakespeare, she had never stopped being fascinated by him. It was going to be a lot of work but it could be done. Then she thought again. It was all right mastering the language; what of the subject matter? She could not keep just writing from memory, just like that, at random. There must be a purpose, there must be a pattern somewhere. She could not find the answers to these questions at the time, but she knew they must be answered before she could write anything publishable. She was not just going to be a writer of ordinary novels. She would have too much competition in that line. She would have to specialize somehow, in some special thing. The only practical knowledge she had was connected with librarianship. You don't go writing about how to file orders or shelve books according to Dewey or the Library of Congress! She could write about the people who came to borrow books, but she had to know about them. What discipline teaches people about people? Psychology? Sociology? Anthropology or history? She knew about the others, but what does a sociologist study? She would ask Francis. He ought to know. She would let him read the manuscript first, then she would ask, 'Where do you learn about people and what do they learn in sociology?'

She told Francis about *The Bride Price* in the evenin. But he replied that he would rather watch *The Saint* on the new television which they had hired. Adah pleaded, and wailed at him that it was good, that her friends at the library said so. He should please read it. She said that Bill thought it should be typed out, because it was good.

Then Francis said, 'You keep forgetting that you are a woman and that you are black. The white man can barely tolerate us men, to say nothing of brainless females like you who could think of nothing except how to breast-feed her baby.'

'That may be so,' cried Adah, 'but people have read it. And they say it is good. Just read it, I want your opinion. Don't you know what it means to us if in the future I could be a writer?'

Francis laughed. What ever was he going to hear next? A woman writer in his own house, in a white man's country?

'Well, Flora Nwapa is black and she writes,' Adah challenged.

'Flora Nwapa writes her stuff in Nigeria,' Francis rejoined.

'I have seen her books in all the libraries where I worked.'

Francis did not reply to this. He was not going to read Adah's rubbish and that was that. Adah was hurt badly, but she said nothing. She simply took her notebooks of 'rubbish' and placed them neatly where she kept the books she had borrowed from the library that week. She would save up somehow and buy herself a typewriter, a second-hand one, one of those sold at the Crescent, and then she would type it all out. Meanwhile, she would keep them there and go on reading.

The thought of all this haunted her like a bad dream. That Francis would not read her book was bad enough but that he had called it rubbish without doing so was a deeper hurt, and that he had said that she would never be a writer because she was black and because she was a woman was like killing her spirit. She felt empty. What else was there for her to do now? It was plain to her that Francis could never tolerate an intelligent woman. She blamed herself again. They ought not to have come, then she would not have had this urge to write now; her marriage would have been saved, at least for the time being, because she knew that some time later she was going to write. Librarianship was to her simply a stepping stone to bring her nearer to the books which she dreamt she was going to write in the future, when she was forty.

But in England, she had been made to start almost twenty years before her time. Her books might not be published until she was forty, but her story had been completed. She could not go back now. She had known the feeling she had when she finished the story, she had tasted the fulfilment of seeing others read her work, and had felt an inner glow that was indescribable when other people said how much they had enjoyed reading it. Peggy had said, 'It was so funny, I could not put it down. It was so comical.' Bill had said, 'You only, and nobody else, could have written that.' Well, there was no going back now. She must go forward.

The following Saturday she left the children with Francis and dashed to the Crescent to do her week-end shopping. They were all sleeping, Francis and the children, and she did not bother to wake them up. The day was wet. The queues at the Crescent were endless. Adah had to queue for meat, for ground rice, for semolina, and even okra had to be queued for. She had to stand, here and there, all over the place in the dripping rain. In the end, she was happy to rush home, all wet but with a sense of relief that her shopping had all been done very early in the morning before the children were awake.

As she approached their landing she could smell the odour of burning paper. She ran inside quickly, hoping and praying that Vicky had not set their room on fire. But inside, she saw that Vicky and the others were still asleep. It was Francis standing there by the stove, burning the paper. He saw her come in, her wet face demanding an explanation. But Francis went on burning the paper. They seldom talked to each other, the two of them. Not being able to bear the smell any longer, Adah had to speak.

She said, 'But, Francis, could you not have thrown all those papers you are burning into the dusbin, instead of creating this awful smell in the room?'

'I was afraid you'd dig them out of the bin. So I had to burn them,' was the prompt reply.

Adah became curious, suspicious, her heart beating faster. 'What are they, Francis? What are you burning? Letters? Who wrote them? Francis, what are you burning?'

Francis did not reply for a while, but went on feeding crumpled sheets into the stove and watching the burnt papers flying lifelessly about the room like black birds. He blocked Adah's view on purpose with his broad back.

Adah knew that posture of Francis's, standing there, challenging her. When he turned his face round, she knew she had seen that triumphant smile on his face before. Now she remembered. She had seen him smile like that when he was telling her how successful he had been in killing a monkey belonging to his friend. The friend had kept this monkey as a pet, to the annoyance of everybody. Francis had bought rat poison, smeared it on a piece of bread and given it to the monkey. The monkey had died, but the agony it went through, twisting in pain, the mournful cry of the unfortunate animal, had never ceased to delight Francis. He had told this story to Adah so many times, garnished with gruesome demonstrations, that Adah never forgot the way he smiled when telling it. There was another terrible story he had told Adah, smiling just like he was doing now. It was the story of a goat which his father had bought for Christmas. The goat was tied up in the back yard, and Francis got the strongest horse-whip he could find, and started to lash this goat, telling it to tell him what two times two was. Adah had asked him whether it did not bother him, whipping some animal that could neither talk nor know what two times two was. Francis would then smile and smack his little lips, his bright eyes glistening behind his spectacles, and tell her that it did not matter at all, what mattered was that the goat would not answer his questions, so he had to be whipped for it. Adah remembered the whipping she got from her Cousin Vincent, and she would remember how each stroke went burning into her skin, and would shudder and tell Francis she did not want to listen to stories about his 'heroic conquests'.

Now Francis had that sickly smile on his face, and Adah

guessed that he was smug with some heroic deed. He picked up the last sheet, and among the crumpled papers she saw the orange cover of one of the exercise books in which she had written her story. Then reality crashed into her mind. Francis was burning her story; he had burned it all. The story that she was basing her dream of her becoming a writer upon. The story that she was going to show Titi and Vicky and Bubu and baby Dada when they grew up. She was going to tell them, she was going to say, 'Look, I wrote that when I was a young woman with my own hand and in the English language.' And she was sure they were all going to laugh and their children were going to laugh too and say, 'Oh, Granny, you are so funny.'

Then she said to Francis, her voice small and tired, 'Bill called that story my brainchild. Do you hate me so much, that you could kill my child? Because that is what you have done.'

'I don't care if it is your child or not. I have read it, and my family would never be happy if a wife of mine was permitted to write a book like that.'

'And so you burnt it?'

'Can't you see that I have?'

That to Adah was the last straw. Francis could kill her child. She could forgive him all he had done before, but not this.

She got a new job at the British Museum as a library officer. Francis gave up his job because he guessed that Adah was now earning a great deal more than she had ever done in the past. But Adah remained adamant to her resolution. Her money was for herself and her children.

Life with Francis became purgatorial after that. She was back into the street once more, surrounded by children just like the Pied Piper, looking for a house to live in. It took a long time, but she eventually got a two-room flat which she had to share with rats and cockroaches.

Francis would not let her take anything with her: noise and fighting was so great that the police had to be called in. The landlady apologized to her later, and said, 'I am sorry I called the police, but he was going to kill you, you know.' The policewoman who came ordered Francis to relinquish a box of clothes for the children.

So Adah walked to freedom, with nothing but four babies, her new job and a box of rags. Not to worry, she had not sustained many injuries apart from a broken finger and swollen lips. She was treated at the Archway Hospital. Francis's parting words were that if Adah thought he was coming to see her and her brats, then he would rather she started thinking of him as a bastard.

Adah was happy about this; she did not want to see him again, never on this earth.

But things got awful for Adah. A month later, she discovered she was pregnant again. In fact she had been pregnant for three months, through all those fights, and to cap it all, Francis traced their new address through the children. He followed Titi and Vicky on their way home from school.

One day, Adah was at her wits' end, wondering what she was going to do now, when a tap on her window sent her peering through the glass. It was Francis who, not realizing that Adah had seen him, started to bash on the window as if he were going to break it. Adah was frightened now. She had lied to the landlord that her husband had gone home to Nigeria and that he would send for them soon when he was fully settled at home. She had to speak all this in Yoruba otherwise she would not have got the flat. When she signed the cheque she gave the landlord he had noticed the name and had said, 'How come a nice girl like you got married to a YAIMIRIN?' *Yaimirin* and *ajeyon*, are the two words the Ibos are known by – it means a race of cannibals. Adah had told him that it was a case of childish infatuation. But she silenced him by paying him six weeks in advance, and by cheque as well. This impressed the man, and bought Adah her freedom for a while.

But now, Francis was bashing at the window and it would be only a question of time before the landlord and the landlady would know that her husband was in London and that she was Ibo as well. Anger welled up inside her, but she opened the door.

The first sentence that came to her mouth was: 'I thought you said that you would never come to see us. What are you here for?'

Francis ignored her but forced himself into her room. Adah sensed trouble. Then he said, 'In our country, and among our people, there is nothing like divorce or separation. Once a man's wife, always a man's wife until you die. You cannot escape. You are bound to him.'

Adah nodded but reminded him that, among their people, the husband provides for the family and that a wicked man that knocked his wife about ran the risk of losing her altogether.

'My father knocked my mother about until I was old enough to throw stones at him. My mother never left my father.'

'Yes,' agreed Adah again, 'but was there a month when your father did not pay the rent, give food money, pay for all your school fees? Can you, Francis, show me some vests or anything these children can lay their hands upon which you can claim to have bought for them? No, Francis, you broke the laws of our people first, not me. And remember, Francis, I am not your mother. I am me, and I am different from her. It is a mistake to use your mother as a yardstick. You never loved or respected her. You simply tolerated her, I know that now, because it never crossed your mind to work and send her money like other Nigerian students do. That should have warned me. In the short courting period we had I noticed that you never thought of giving her anything. It was always you, you all the time and she, poor soul, was always giving and giving to you. To her nothing is too much, no human is good enough for you. You remember the saying that a man who treated his mother like a shit would always treat his wife like a shit? That should have warned me, but I was too blind to see then.'

What followed is too horrible to print. Adah remembered, though, that during the confusion Francis told her he had a knife. He now carried knives with him. She tried several times to call for help, but could feel the life being squeezed out of her. She then heard people talking, banging the door which Francis had locked. But the landlord had guessed that Francis was Adah's husband and, like most of his people, he didn't want to interfere until a real murder had been committed. It was an old Irish man living on the top floor,

Devlin was his name, who broke the door open.

This could not go on, Adah told herself when everybody had gone. She had left Francis over four weeks before, she did not ask for any maintenance either for herself or for the children. She had to pay almost forty pounds a month for the children at the nursery and for their dinner money and to a girl to take Titi and Vicky across the road. She had to pay almost the same amount for the rent, to say nothing of the fact that most of her everyday clothes, their cooking utensils, even the spoons and the children's vitamin coupons and the family allowances were all with him. Now he came here adding this insult to all the injuries he had caused. Adah threw caution to the wind. One never knew; Francis was carrying a knife today, she told herself – he did use it to threaten her, but she had been so bruised and maltreated that she could not see herself going to work for a week or two. No, the law must step in.

Then she looked round the room and saw with tears the radiogram she had just bought with a little deposit off the man at the Crescent; she saw it had been smashed by Francis. She saw the new teaset she was paying for from the landlady's catalogue all broken, the flowery pattern looking pathetically dislocated. No, she needed protection against this type of destruction.

Adah had never been to a court before in all her life. All she wanted was for the magistrate or the judge, or whoever it was, to ask Francis to stay away from her and her children. She was not suing for maintenance, she did not even know if she was entitled to any. She simply wanted her safety, and protection for the children. The wife of the Indian doctor, who was a doctor herself, and who had treated her, had said: 'Next time you might not be so lucky with a man who can beat you like this.' She gave her two weeks off work and told her to spend most of it in bed.

Inside the courtroom Adah started to stammer. The doctor had told her to call her and that she would come to give evidence. Adah had thanked her, but did not call her. Suppose they found Francis guilty of assault which was what they were charging him with? What then would she gain by it?

They might send him to prison, and what good would t
to her?

She should not have worried because Francis showed another side to his character which she had not seen before. All
the bruises and cuts and bumps Adah had to show the court
were the result of falls. Yes, he broke her radiogram because
he thought it was a chair. He would pay for the repairs.
Nobody asked him how he was going to pay, since he was
jobless.

Adah did not know that they would require so many
details. She had never read Law or anything to do with Law,
but it was one of Francis's major subjects. Adah hated courts
from that day on. Another thing shook her further.

The magistrate said the children had to be maintained, and
since Adah had always been the head of the family financially
she was given the custody of the children. But how much
could Francis afford?

Francis said they had never been married. He then asked
Adah if she could produce the marriage certificate. Adah
could not. She could not even produce her passport and the
children's birth certificates. Francis had burnt them all. To
him, Adah and the kids ceased to exist. Francis told her this
in court in low tones in their own language.

It was then the magistrate knew he was dealing with a very
clever person. He said, 'You can say the children are not
your own, but you have to contribute to their maintenance.
She just can't do it all on her own.'

Francis replied, 'I don't mind their being sent for adoption.'

Something happened to Adah then. It was like a big hope
and a kind of energy charging into her, giving her so much
strength even though she was physically ill with her fifth
child. Then she said very loud and very clear, 'Don't worry,
sir. The children are mine, and that is enough. I shall never
let them down as long as I am alive.'

She walked out from that court at Clerkenwell and wandered anywhere, not seeing anything, tears flowing from her
eyes without stopping, her temperature rising. She never
fully recovered from the Big Fight. She arrived in Camden
Town, in front of a butcher's shop where they sold cheap
chickens. She stood there, not because she was buying any

191

chicken but because she was tired, hungry but without appetite, and feeling like being sick. The tears still flowed.

Then a voice cut through the crowd, called her by her Ibo
pet-name 'Nne nna'. The first thought that struck her was that
she was dying, because nobody had called her by that name
except people who knew her as a little girl, and only her Pa
used to call her like that, drawing out every syllable. The
voice was very near now and it called again. A man's voice,
much too deep to be her Pa's and too gentle to be Francis's.

Then she saw the face of the man. Then she remembered,
and he remembered. He was a friend she used to know a very,
very long time before, when she was at the Girls' High. His
eyes swept down and saw the ring on her finger and he said:
'So you married Francis?'

She replied that she had.

It was like Fate intervening. It was like a story one might
read in a true story magazine. This old friend of Adah's paid
for the taxi that took her home from Camden Town because
he thought she was still with her husband.